UNDER THE NORSE STAR

Tales & Legends for Reluctant Readers

Book 2
Feathers of the Phoenix

UNDER THE NORSE STAR

Cheryl Carpinello

Silver Quill Publishing

Published in Print and Ebook format by Silver Quill Publishing 2025

Print ISBN: 978-1-80440-133-0
ebook ISBN: 978-1-80440-132-3

First Print Edition 2025
First Ebook Edition 2025

Photos by Wendy Leighton-Porter, Dreamstime
Cover © Berge Design
Edited by Nancy M. Bell
Map by Connor Hegge
Layout and Production by Typesetting Books

A special thanks to my grandson Connor for consenting, if a bit reluctantly, to draw the map!

This has been too long in coming. My apologizes and thanks to all those readers who consistently inquired as to how it was coming. It's Here!

OTHER WORKS BY CHERYL CARPINELLO

EARLY READERS

Grandma/Grandpa's Tales 1: Wild Creatures in my Neighborhood and What If I Went to the Circus

Grandma/Grandpa's Tales 2: Singers of Songs and The Not Too Stubborn Humpback Whale

Grandma/Grandpa's Tales 3: Vampires in the Backyard and A Fish Tale

BOOKS IN THE TALES AND LEGENDS FOR RELUCTANT READERS SERIES

Tutankhamen Speaks (Lexile Level: 840L)

Sons of the Sphinx (Lexile Level: 620L HL)

Feathers of the Phoenix: The Atlantean Horse, Book 1

Guinevere: On the Eve of Legend, Book 1 (Lexile Level: 750L)

Guinevere: At the Dawn of Legend, Book 2 (Lexile Level: 750L)

Guinevere: The Legend, Book 3 (Lexile Level: 660L)

The King's Ransom, Young Knights of the Round Table (Lexile Level: 720L)

SHORT STORIES

Guardian of a Princess & Other Shorts

PRAISE FOR CHERYL CARPINELLO'S BOOKS

"Fans of mythology and fast-paced quests will find this a worthy continuation of the story, leaving them eager for the next "Feather" in the series."

—*Wendy Leighton-Porter, author*

"Author Cheryl Carpinello creates a mysterious and entertaining adventure about the ancient mythological tale of Atlantis."

—*The KBReview*

"... adventure, fantasy, and mythology, all packed into a quick read--perfect for kids who find "fat books" intimidating."

—*Michelle, Amazon*

"I liked the storyline and it definitely sets up for future adventures in the series."

—*Jamie, Amazon*

"Taking legend, ancient mythology, and the mystery of a sunken city, Atlantis, the author weaves an engaging and exciting tale that will attract even the most reluctant reader."

—*Emily-Jane Hills Orford, Readers' Favorite*

"This is an excellent adventure...Cheryl Carpinello writes exciting contemporary language for the more reluctant older (reader)."

—*Jemima Pett, UK*

"Fast-paced and exciting, the storyline keeps you right on the edge of your seat..."

—*Clio, Amazon UK*

Long before humans,
mystical beings inhabited this isle.
And though not often seen, they are still here.
And long ago, far above, the Norse star watched all.
Now in your time, it is known as the North Star.

—*Njal, the Ancient One*

Thou hast beheld all that has been,
hast witnessed the passing of the ages.
Thou knowest when it was that the
waves of the sea rose and o'erflowed the rocks...

—*Claudian, Phoenix*

TABLE OF CONTENTS

MORE ABOUT:

ᚾᛈ ᛗᛁᛉᛋ ᛬ ᛈᛋᚻᛗᛉᛋᛏᛃᛋ

OF THE FIVE FEATHERS:

**One was kept close to the one who survived.
One was sent north to the Old Gods.
One was sent into the fires of Hephaestus.
One was sent to the land of the Druids.
One was sent to the land of the Pharaohs.**

POSEIDON'S JUDGEMENT

Poseidon, saddened his test of the Atlanteans' compassion failed, destroyed the island. The citizens felt the ground tremble. Shining white buildings cracked and fell. The once-smooth ground covered with the greenest of grass heaved and coughed. The sea lapped at the newly made canals and started to swallow the land and the people. Before long, nothing could be found of the city prized above all others by Poseidon. It was as if it had never been. Poseidon saved only two things, for even creatures, innocent as they were, suffered the same fate. One was a white stallion he spirited to an island far away and turned to stone. The creature tried to resist, but Poseidon was too strong. The other thing he saved: Five Golden Red Feathers from the Phoenix. These floated to the top of the ocean above where Atlantis sank. With a sad breath, Poseidon blew those into the air where they flew until landing on five distant shores.

POSEIDON'S PROMISE

Poseidon promised that when the time was right, when compassion once again ruled the people, the Phoenix's Feathers would be united with the stallion, and the island of Atlantis would raise from the depths of the ocean. At that time, all of its people, the Phoenix, and the white stallion would be able to return home.

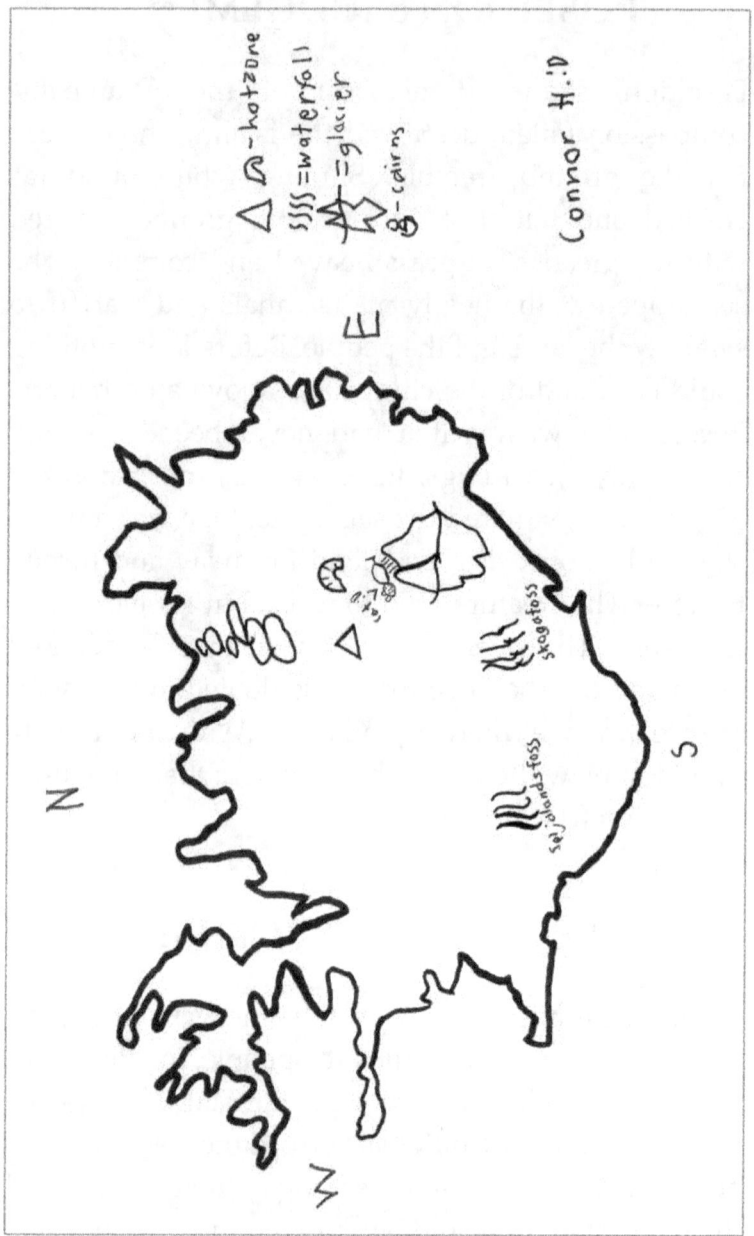

△ ⌂ -hot zone
ЅЅЅЅ =waterfall
⋀⋀ =glacier
Ȣ -cairns

Connor H.'D

PROLOGUE

Off in the distance, calving ice trembles and explodes, bouncing off granite, sending ocean waves crashing across the northern fjords of Eyjafjordur. Puffins flee into the cloudless sky. Killer whales expose their white bellies as they leap in the air and dive deep into the reverberating blue ocean to escape. And always the stench of rotten eggs makes its way across the water to the land beyond.

Just beyond the horizon, beneath the ofttimes frozen earth, molten lava courses. Continually through light and dark, it forges a way through millennium old glaciers, melting a pathway through the volcanic rock. Sharp, red hot surfaces create vents the liquid fire rises through, filling the air with odorous sulfur. Gaseous clouds form inches above the ground, fatal to any invaders, and wind their way up my valleys bounded by basalt cliffs

Still further yet across its width, mountains tremble, shake, cry, and break as the Earth-fire comes alive. Thunderous roars fill the air, twisting trees, crashing rocks, splitting the earth. More caustic odors flow from newly missing mountain crowns. Fiery liquids flow down those sides further reshaping the terrain and carving out deep furrows. Immense heat incinerates all it touches: vegetation, trees, and ice. The mountains keep belching, sending scorching lava faster and faster down the slopes. Soon entire valleys disappear beneath hot, red glows. As night approaches, the mountains cough and quietly go to sleep. In the cool of late night and early morning, fires burn out, leaving blackened lava rock on the earth. Steaming vapors find a way through and curl up into small clouds hanging just inches from the burnt ground. Protecting and watching.

ᚤᚼᛂᚼᛐᚼ

Long before the dawn of civilization, before today's world took shape, this island stood here. Long before humans set foot on its shores and rocky landscape, beings lived here. Mystical beings which guarded and protected this isle.

Always this isle is guarded. Land Spirits (Landvaettir) watch. In the North, a massive Griffin roams. A Fire Breathing Dragon guards the East. The South sits under the all-seeing eye of a Giant who stands taller than the trees. In the West, an enormous bull watches for danger. My guardians, forever on duty, ensure the safety of our home. I oversee them all.

And above all, long before names were given, long before humans knew of them, heavenly stars lit this northern world. Given names by the Norsemen, these guiding stars brought far away travelers to these shores. Today, some call them by different names, but one is always known by the same name: the Norse Star. This star and others still shine, in the light and in the dark, upon this land adding mystery to the magical. These beings watch closely even over me.

This is my home.
I am the Gyrfalcon. Greatest of Strength and Speed.
I am the Land of Fire and Ice.
I am Iceland.

But once, from centuries far removed, a simple golden red
Feather floated down and hid itself here. And now danger
threatens all.

CHAPTER 1

IT'S TIME

Standing here in my backyard, a slight breeze ruffles my blond hair with its emerald streak, my tribute to the queen who showed me the value of Nana's gift. Some days I still wonder at the power given to me by Nana, a gift that she held close to her heart for decades. To hear the dead and actually talk with them is not something she took lightly. And neither do I ... most of the time.

I breathe deeply, and my whole body energizes as the invigorating air fills my lungs. It's crisp and cool and so welcome after summer. Even though I'm more than ready for spring after our snowy, cold winters, fall always refreshes my body and my spirit.

I love Colorado in the fall. The changing colors of the leaves start now with the cooler nights. Deep and light greens give way to brilliant yellows, burning oranges, and blazing reds. Nature's way of welcoming winter. As the winds increase, leaves float down to the ground, building up so thick in places it's like walking on cushions.

Spending several days in Egypt with King Tut, almost two years ago, cured me of any fondness I had for the sun. The intense heat, the sweat running down my body, the struggle to breathe at times, I decided all that was best left behind.

I touch the golden ankh hanging around my neck, embracing this gift from King Tut and his queen Ankhesenamun after reuniting them in death. Sometimes I still find it impossible to believe that I freely, if a bit reluctantly, gave my hand to a ghost to transport me back to 1330 BC. ancient Egypt! I've heard voices of the dead for years, but never felt the presence of one within my soul as I did with Ankhesenamun.

Shivers still run through me when I think about the time wrap that Tut used to transport us back in time. The nausea and cold sweat. My world spinning out of control. Stars zipping across my vision. Suddenly, finding myself in the palace where he and Hesena, his boyhood name for her, grew up. Where they found out that Tut's father had a zoo. Where Tut's father Akhenaten first acknowledged him as his son. Where I first saw the Window of Appearances. Where my world, my real world, changed forever.

I remember our struggle to find Ay and the secret to Hesena's burial. The clues hidden on the stella at the Sphinx, on the walls of Tut's and Ay's tombs, and the mystery in the hills above Akhen-Aten. The cave where I thought I would die by Horemheb's hand! The same cave that became my Window of Appearances. Where I received the Golden Ankh from Tut and Hesena.

And it is because of that deed, we, my cousin Jerome and I, were called on to help raise Atlantis so its people still living here could return home.

Jerome, well, he discovered his gift on our visit to Grandpa on Telendos. One neither of us knew he possessed. His ability to hear and talk to the Atlantean Horse statue on Telendos just by touching it surprised all of us. But I still wonder whether Grandpa always knew, and if that was why he invited both of us to visit him in June, on the Sun Day, to recover the first Feather of the Phoenix. A task entrusted to me by the ancient Atlantean. And then later by Grandpa.

I still remember his words: *We're descendants of Atlantis.*

And his answer when we asked why no one in our family ever spoke of this:

Your parents have never spoken of this to you because they are not aware. There's a lot of magic in this world. Magic that people choose to not believe in because it's easier that way. The ability to hear voices from the past is not shared by all in the family.

My grandfather passed the information about our heritage down to me. Neither my father nor my mother ever knew. They didn't hear, but I did, and so did your Nana.

And now, so do I. I've always been a bit of a dreamer and believer in magic. I mean, I even believe in unicorns. Believe that they are somewhere in our world today. Do you?

As for Jerome, I'm not sure that he fully believes in magic, even after Telendos. He definitely doesn't believe in unicorns. At least not yet! He's more of a concrete thinker. Me, not so much!

Tomorrow is the Autumnal Equinox. No sign or word from Grandpa or the Atlantean visitor about retrieving the next Feather. Surprising, but nothing I can do. Besides, we're both in school. No way our folks will agree to a visit to Grandpa.

Checking my watch, I head inside to finish drying the pans. I want to be done when Jerome gets back from conditioning and comes for our run around the lake which is a few blocks from our houses. We live across the street from each other. He's a wrestler and already spends an hour each day in the weight room at school getting ready for the season which starts in November. He hopes to take state this year as a sophomore.

The pan I pick up drips on the floor. Putting it aside, I grab a paper towel to clean up the water… and stop. Something's happening. My skin's tingling. The ankh around my neck pulses softly.

Hello, Rosa.

CHAPTER 2

MNESEUS

I knock the pan to the floor, watch it bounce on the tile, the clatter ringing in my ears as I turn around. I stare unable to speak for what seems like several minutes.

My brain explodes. The ringing's not from the pan, but from the voices crying out in my head. I clasp my hands over my ears in an attempt to block them.

He's here! In my kitchen! It's as if I conjured him up just by thinking of the Phoenix Feathers.

Grasping the Ankh, I steady myself and give him an awkward smile. The ancient Atlantean looks different from when I first encountered him. Instead of his previous dark blue tunic and lightweight power blue pants, a heavy red coat, zippered up to his chin, reaches past his knees. A hood covers his head. Heavy royal blue pants protect his legs. On his feet, regular shoes have replaced the sandals.

I do not understand your weather. I dressed for the ice.

"Sorry." I offer him a paper towel. Sweat is beginning to run down his face. "For your face. You should also unzip your coat and remove the hood from your head.

You'll be cooler."

Thank you.

He removes his hood revealing damp brown hair. After wiping his face, I take the paper towel from him and put it in the trash.

I did not introduce myself properly before. In my home I'm called Mneseus.

I struggle with the pronunciation. "Mne...Mnes..."

He repeats it for me. "Mneseus."

Listening carefully, I get it this time. "Mneseus. Does it have a special meaning?"

My name is given to one whom others come to for counsel or advice. It is an honorable name. I'm not the first to have it. Many others carried it before me.

I wait to hear what he's come to say, although I'm pretty sure I already know.

It's time. Time to collect the next Feather. The Sun Day is tomorrow.

"I know, but we can't go now. We're in school. Jerome's at practice. Our parents will never let us visit Grandpa now." In a bit of a panic, I look at my watch and realize Jerome won't be home for at least another 30 minutes.

You don't have to visit Simon. Have you forgotten Tut's way?

My stomach turns over at that. OMG. Forgotten? Not hardly. Even though I've tried.

"But, the Horse?"

My instructions from it are clear. I'm to send you and Jerome to the land of Fire and Ice. Since long before your time, the Norse Star guarded, and still guards, that land and the beings there who call it home. It also guards the Feather. Once you have the Feather, I'll take you to the Horse. No time will pass in your world.

"But..."

I will return at three hours past dawn for you and Jerome.

"But..."

Do not worry, Rosa. No one will know you are gone.

Before I can protest, he simply disappears, leaving only the frightened voices in my head.

ᚠᚺᚾᛋᚲᛈᛁᚴ

After sending a text to Jerome, I'm sitting at the kitchen table waiting and wondering how in the world my life got this crazy. First, ancient Egypt with a ghost. Then Telendos, a small island in the Mediterranean hardly anyone has ever heard of. And now, to an Iceland of eons ago! Obviously, it wasn't enough that the Pharaoh Horemheb nearly succeeding in killing me in the cave at Akhen-Aten. Or, that John King, one of the Four Horsemen, would have shot me outside the cave on Telendos if Nikos hadn't pushed me out of the way and taken the bullet himself.

I'm not an idiot! You'd think I would have learned by now to say no. But I remember the difference I made in Tut and Hesena's afterlives. And the difference in my own life knowing that Nana's gift is just that: a gift. It's because of that journey to Ancient Egypt, that I can't say no when someone needs my special gift. And then there's the voices, ever present, crying out for help.

CHAPTER 3

NOT ME!

"Hey Rosa," Jerome calls as he comes in the back door.

He's sweating as much as Mneseus. His gray t-shirt's soaked. Water's dripping down his face from his red hair. Unfortunately, that workout smell follows him in.

"Couldn't you shower before leaving practice?" I pinch my nose and wave my hand trying to clear the air.

Ignoring me, he opens the fridge and grabs a bottle of water. Unscrewing the top, he takes a long drink. "I got your text. Sounded like I should get here right away. What's up?"

"Mneseus."

"What? What's a Mneseus?" He presses the cold bottle against his cheeks, still flushed from his workout and running over here.

"The ancient Atlantean."

Jerome almost drops the open water bottle. "Where is he? What does he want?" He breathes deeply a couple of times and runs his fingers through his damp red hair.

"Tomorrow's the autumnal equinox." I pause, waiting maybe for him to make the connection.

"And?"

"It's a Sun Day. Time to find the next Feather."

Jerome pulls a chair out from the table and plops down.

"Really? You know," he says, "even though we've talked about our visit to Grandpa, and about Nikos getting shot, and finding that Feather in the caves, it still seems unreal most of the time."

"I know, but it's not." I sit back down next to him. "He'll be back early tomorrow to get us."

We both look at the clock—7 pm.

"Rosa, I can't go. I have two workouts scheduled for tomorrow. One's with the team. I can't, won't, miss that."

He holds up his hand as I start to talk.

"We can't go. What would our folks say? They'll never let us go, especially with someone they don't know, someone who doesn't exist, someone who's dead."

He puts his still sweaty hand in my face again.

"Nope. We can't go."

Grabbing his grossly moist hand, I push it away, then wipe my hand on my jeans.

"Listen," I say more sternly than I actually feel. "No time will pass here. No one will even know we're gone."

"Really, Rosa? Really? Just how is that possible?" His eyebrows arch, and his eyes flash mirroring the sarcasm in his voice as he waits for me to answer.

Now it's my turn to take a deep breath.

"Well, he's going to use the Time Wrap that Tut used with me. No time passes here, but time moves forward wherever we go. It's weird, but it works. Tut proved that to me. At least it did work that way the last time." I grasp the golden ankh around my neck.

"Really? That Time Wrap thing you told Grandpa and me about?"

I nod.

"And no time passes here?"

I nod again.

"And I'll be here to go to practice tomorrow afternoon?"

I nod a third time.

"You're sure?"

"Yes, unless we die there."

The color drains from his face. I smile at him.

"Trust me, Jerome."

With a shake of his head, he starts toward the door, stops, and just stands there. I've seen him do this before when a thought he can't shake strikes him.

Slowly I reach out and touch his arm.

No emotion shows on his face. It's as if his facial features have frozen.

"Jerome?"

"Rosa, have you ever asked yourself..."

He stops mid-sentence.

"Asked what?"

"Asked why you, why me, why we're doing this?" He pauses.

"All the time. In fact, the entire time I was waiting

for you to get here."

"And what kind of an answer did you come up with?"

"None. None at all."

"Rosa, you were almost killed outside that cave on Telendos! Would have been if Nikos hadn't pushed you out of the way. Hadn't taken the bullet meant for you. Not to mention if King had fired again and gotten me also."

I sit back down, and Jerome does the same. I rest my chin on my hands. Closing my eyes to block out my world, I hear the voices. Voices crying out in terror, in fear, in pain. And I know.

"It's because of them, the Atlanteans." I shake my head slowly to stop him from interrupting. "They're crying out to me to help them. I heard them the first time he came here in the spring. They're always in my head. I can't ignore them. Trust me, I've tried in the past. They know I hear them; know I can't *not* help them. I learned that with Tut."

"I know about the voices, Rosa. You've told me about them. That's not what I'm talking about."

"Then what?"

"Why Grandpa? What's his role in all this?"

"I don't know, except he wants to help because he, we, somehow are related to the ancient Atlanteans. I mean, it sounds crazy, but he believes it. And I guess, so do I ... sort of."

Jerome slowly shakes his head as he gets up and again walks to the door. "Remember the reason he moved to that island after Grandma's death?"

"He said he wanted to go home." I fall silent.

"Yeah, but what's home for him, Rosa?"

Without another word, he walks out and leaves me just sitting here wondering what he was trying to say.

CHAPTER 4

READY, SET, GONE

For at least the twentieth time, I look at the clock on the small table beside my bed. Five-thirty. Groaning, I drag myself to a sitting position and eventually crawl out of bed. Didn't sleep much last night. Tossed and turned. I wouldn't call it excitement that kept sleep at bay. More like fear, but not quite. The two times I actually fell asleep, I woke up sweating and breathing like I'd just run a marathon, which I've never done. Each time, I'd been near a cave. Couldn't be a co-incidence, not when that was the case in Egypt and in Telendos. Each time I managed to stay alive. But if this trip back to early Iceland involves another cave, what are my chances of beating fate a third time? No, not fear, more of a healthy concern. A very healthy concern! And Jerome's thoughts about Grandpa kept my brain much too busy to sleep as well.

A soft tap on my window interrupts my thoughts. Jerome's here. I open the blinds and give him a thumbs up. Throwing on my clothes, jeans, long sleeve shirt, and hiking boots, I grab my parka and, with my hand on the doorknob, stop. On my desk chair is my backpack containing the pouch to protect the Feather when we find it. Can't forget that. Reaching over, I grab it and leave my room.

Jerome's waiting just outside the back door.

He greets me with a nod of his head. "Well, guess we're ready to do this." His hand sweeps down my clothes and his. "Hope none of our neighbors are curious this morning. Be a little hard to explain why we're dressed like this when it's already nearly seventy degrees."

I laugh, a little nervous. "I know. Pretty sure it's not going to be this warm in Iceland. It's not that far from the Arctic Circle."

"Twenty-five miles from the northernmost point and two hundred from the capital of Reykjavik. More or less."

"Wow, do a little research last night?"

"Yeah, after leaving here. And, after showering."

His subtle reference to last night coaxes a smile from my nervous self.

"The winds are also said to swirl around the Arctic Circle like a banshee all year round."

"Iceland never gets very warm, not like Telendos or Egypt." I lift my blond hair off my neck. Sweat's starting to run down my back. "Hope Mneseus gets here soon."

"You're sure no one will know we're gone?"

I nod. "One hundred percent."

Greetings, Rosa. Jerome.

We both jump. Darn, I wish he wouldn't keep

sneaking up on us like that.

"Where did you come from?" Jerome asks.

Mneseus looks toward the sky.

"Right," Jerome answers sarcastically.

I jab him with my elbow.

Are you ready?

"Yes," we both say.

Jerome squeezes my hand.

Take my hand.

We each take one of his hands.

"Hold on to your stomach, Jerome."

"Really?"

I nod, and my world spins as stars fly past my vision.

ᚱᚢᛏᛖ ᛋᚢᛈᛂ ᚷᚨᛏᛉ

Strangers are coming to my land. Searching for an Ancient One. My land is filled with Ancient Ones: Trolls, Elves, Ghosts. There are many more, but these intruders come for the Ancient One which can lead them to a treasure hidden under the Norse Star. A treasure we have long protected. A treasure that offers death and rebirth. A treasure many seek at all costs. I fear for my land and my protectors.

CHAPTER 5

STRANGE LAND

I grasp my middle in the hopes of calming my stomach and keeping things where they belong. Time Wraps are not fun. It's like I'm on a roller coaster, hanging at the top of a steep track, suspended for just a brief moment before plunging down at breakneck speed. Don't know about you, but my stomach always stays longer at the top. And when it catches up to my body, Look out! Now, like then, waves of nausea and cold sweats sweep over me. I give myself a firm hug hoping that I don't throw up. That would be embarrassing.

Jerome's looking a little green and shaky. He's rubbing his arms slowly. His glance at me is almost one of distrust.

"I told you it would be weird."

"Really, you call this weird?" That sarcastic voice again. He starts to shake his head and stops.

I totally understand. Any excess movement is a killer until the body becomes stable.

It's warmer than I expected. A small breeze cools my face. The air smells clean and fresh, not like at home where you inhale car fumes and sometimes smoke from fireplaces, and sadly from forest fires. The ground is littered with boulders of all sizes.

"Any idea where in Iceland we are?" Jerome asks, looking around us.

His stomach must have calmed down.

"Not a clue," I answer. All around us rise peaks of different sizes. Some covered in snow, some bare, and some covered in ice. "We might be able to see more if we climb up that mountain." I point to the mountain directly in front of us.

"Good idea, although it looks to be quite a hike."

"I wonder where Mneseus is? Surely he wouldn't just leave us here?"

We both turn around searching for Mneseus, but we're the only living beings around. That's not to say that Mneseus isn't living, but, well, you understand.

Then, as if coming out of the deep blue heavens, we hear his voice.

Seek the Ancient One. Guided by the Norse Star, the Ancient One will lead you into the past to find the Feather.

"Well," Jerome says, "that gives us no directions." He shakes his head in disbelief. "Guess we just head for that mountain," he adds.

"Right," I say, more than a little disappointed at the lack of direction from Mneseus.

We set off, eager to find the One who can help us. The way is not smooth. Mossy rocks litter our path making walking difficult. We both stumble a few times. Not sure how long our time here is. I've got a feeling that the longer we're here, the more nervous Jerome will be about getting back home.

Strange land, this Iceland. Barely a sound except for the screeching of the birds overhead. Not sure what those are. They glide over the ground, in graceful arcs, searching for food. Once in a while, one swoops close as if inspecting us as a source of food.

ᛋᛈᚱᛏᛏᚷᛉ

Those are my guardians, Fair One, keeping watch where I cannot. The longer you and your companion are here, the more dangerous my land becomes.

ᚱᛏᛏᛏᛉ

Jerome stops and waits until I catch up. I tend to dawdle.

"How far away does that mountain look, Rosa?"

"I'm not sure we're any closer. And if this ground gets any rougher..."

"I know. I wonder..."

Then he stops, concentrating. I wait patiently. Well, almost. I shift my weight back and forth to keep my feet from getting too cold.

"Look at all these rocks. This isn't natural. It's like a hole just opened in the sky and dropped these. I wonder if these are from a volcanic eruption?"

"I suppose they could be. This is a volcanic island after all."

"I know, the land of fire and ice," he adds, rolling his eyes.

"Like that mountain there, covered in snow," I add.

He walks ahead a bit then, bending down, picks up a hand of small black pebbles.

"And look at these, Rosa. Polished rocks. Black polished stones," he says, as he lets them slowly drop from his hand. He walks further ahead, stops again, and stares.

"What is it?" There's that frozen look again. His concentrated look.

He stoops again and picks up more pebbles, rubbing them between his fingers. His gaze moves from those to the mountain and back several times before he tells me anything.

"Rosa, I don't think that's a mountain ahead of us."

"Sure it is."

"Nope." He shakes his head. "Look at the base of those cliffs."

My eyes follow his outstretched arm.

"See the white streaks?"

I nod.

"That's not a mountain of dirt. That's a mountain of ice...a glacier, Rosa!"

"But all the dirt..."

"That's volcanic ash mixed with dirt gathered as the glacier moves. It's just like I learned in geology class. The mixture is so heavy, it actually pushes the ground in front of it. That's where all these boulders came from. It thrusts them out of the way."

He motions me to follow.

"See all the dirt and moss beyond the boulders?"

I nod.

"That's what's left after the boulders are pushed over the ground. And these polished pebbles? These are pieces of the boulders and smaller rocks that are ground into shiny pieces by the force. Kind of like being put into a rock polisher."

"And over here...hear that?" He runs to the edge of a rushing nearby stream. "This comes from the glacier. It's constantly melting as it moves. Come on."

He's running again. I struggle to keep from tripping over those rocks and boulders as I follow.

"This mountain isn't just a single peak. It's a series of ice hills, each reaching higher. Each melting. That's what this stream is. Melting ice." He bends down and puts his hand in the water. "Ice cold, Rosa. Feel."

Obediently, I squat down beside him and stick my fingers in the water. "It's like ice water!" My gaze moves back to the hills in front of us. I have no more words. I've never imagined such a sight or such a place.

"Come on!"

Jerome's off and running again.

"Let's see what's up that small valley."

"But what about..."

"In a minute," he calls back disappearing around a corner.

When I catch up, I almost run into him. He puts out a hand to steady me. Stunned, I stand beside him. Neither of us speaks. Before us a huge field of ice spreads out and then disappears over the mountain top and into the sky.

CHAPTER 6

THOUSANDS AND THOUSANDS

"This is a glacier, Rosa!"

I start to answer, but a shock runs through me. The ground shifts beneath our feet. I grab onto Jerome to steady myself. He does the same. Fear I haven't felt in a long while thrums through my being. Voices cry in pain. The ankh heats up almost like it's trying to burn me! I cringe as I grab it and lift it off my chest.

"Earthquake!"

"What?"

"That was an earthquake, Rosa."

I nod and shake my head at the same time.

"What is it, Rosa?"

"It's not just the earthquake. I felt something else. There's something else. A presence that doesn't belong here."

"You're sure?"

"Oh, yeah." I open my hand and let the ankh fall. A bright red spot, a small burn, is left on my palm.

Yes, Fair One. You are right. I sense a strange presence in my land. A disturbance. An evil that shouldn't be here.

ᛈᛇᛉᛞᚼᚼᛏᛏᛏᚼ

"That's not possible."

"Possible or not, I think one of the Four Horsemen is here. And that's scarier than earthquakes. We need to find the Ancient One before whatever is here finds us."

Jerome's stare goes right through me, and then his eyes sweep the land around us. He doesn't hesitate. "Okay, where do you think we should go? How do we find the Ancient One in all this?"

Looking around, my eyes rest on what is right in front of us. "How old do you think that glacier is?"

He studies it for a minute. "Thousands and thousands of years old."

"That would make it...

"Ancient," we both say in unison.

CHAPTER 7

ONE STEP

"Now, we just have to figure out a way to up there. I don't see any clear path."

"No," Jerome says. "Neither do I. My guess..."

"Yes?"

"We follow the stream a bit since that's where it starts. And then, then we climb."

I look at the glacier again, and probably not for the last time. "We climb? How do we climb a glacier?"

"For starters, we need to get closer to the base of the ice."

I glare a bit at him. "Closer to the base of the ice? How do we do that?"

"Follow me. I've got an idea."

I watch for a minute as he travels along the icy stream. I look once again at the sheet of ice far ahead and above us. Once more I wonder how I ended up in what could well be an impossible task. Cries echo in my head. Shaking them off, I start after Jerome. I know why I'm here, but I wonder if Nana ever had any idea of where her gift would take me. I also wonder if this gift ever took her on any strange journeys.

"Com'on, Rosa."

"Coming."

Aside from trying to avoid the cluster of broken rocks and chunks of dirt-covered ice in my way, I catch up to Jerome in just a few minutes.

"We have to cross the river," he says, pointing to the path on the other side.

I stare at the log laying across the river. "You mean walk across that log?"

"Yep."

"Wouldn't it be easier to wade across?"

"Only if you don't mind walking in wet boots and socks the rest of the way, wherever that is."

"Or we could just wade across in our bare feet." Bending down, I put my hand in the water. "Okay, it's still like ice. Lead on, fair Jerome, across the raging river!" I salute him.

He glares at me and raises those eyebrows before stepping on the log.

I laugh, and it echoes across the land. Eerie in a way. My way to ease the tension in the air.

As I watch, Jerome carefully puts one foot in front of the other, his arms outstretched to help him balance. He would look like a tightrope walker in different clothes. Close to the end, he jumps to shore and turns to me.

"Throw me the backpack."

Wriggling out of the straps, I give it a couple of swings before heaving it across the river.

Jerome grabs it mid-air and gives me a thumbs up.

Grinning, he yells, "Okay, your turn. Try not to fall in, okay?"

I swallow my retort. Focusing on the log, I gingerly place my right foot down. *You've got this.*

Holding my arms out, I take another step. Okay, I'm on. Just like on the balance beam, except I always fell off. *One foot in front of the other. Take it easy. One foot in front of the other.* Two more steps, and I'm home free.

Suddenly a loud rumble roars from the top of the glacier. Beneath me, ripples form into small waves on the river. Afraid, I look to Jerome. He's staggering to keep his balance. The ground all around us is shaking again, although this time harder. Rocks start falling into the river along with chunks of glacier ice. Big chunks!

"Rosa, hurry!" Jerome rushes toward the log, his arms waving to keep him from falling. "Rosa!"

CHAPTER 8

DANGER AND...LAUGHTER

The log's bouncing up and down. Falling onto the log, my hands and knees grip it to keep me from falling into the icy water. My body's shaking even harder that the ground around me. Rocks are still falling.

"What in the world?" I yell over the crashing and rumbling.

"It's another earthquake! Here, grab on!

I see Jerome's hand reaching for mine. Our eyes meet and hold.

"Com'on, Rosa. Give me your hand. Reach!"

I focus on him and reach my hand out trying not to lose my balance. Glancing up the river, I see a huge something coming down headed right for me!

"Jerome!"

He doesn't answer, but leans out and grabs my hand, yanking me into the air and on to the shore. Rocks dig into my knees and arms as I hit the shaking ground I struggle to breathe. My head hurts. On the river, the something, a large chunk of ice, is almost even with us!

"What in the world?!" I mumble before my vision blurs. Then...

Jerome watches in horror as the ice rushes by, sweeping the log into the water ahead of it.

↑�ᚷᛁR

"Rosa. Rosa!"

I'm in some kind of a fog. Nothing is clear. And I'm shaking! Hard!

"Rosa!"

OMG! Did I get hit by that ice?

"Rosa! Wake up!"

Icy water hits my face. Choking, I struggle out of the fog. If I'm drowning, I want to see it!

A hand on my back pushes me into sitting position. My vision clears.

"Jerome?"

"Yes. The earthquake's over, I think."

"That was so much stronger than the first one."

"Yes. And probably not the last. This one sent a ton a rocks and ice down from the glacier.

He sits down next to me. "We've barely spent any time here, and already we're in danger. And, there may be more quakes. My God, Rosa. What is it about this quest? What's making it so dangerous no matter where we are?"

I shake my head, wincing as pain shoots through it. "I don't know. I just know danger seems to be everywhere."

Around us echoes laughter. Wicked laughter.

"Jerome..."

A swift shake of his head stops my next words. "I heard. Can't believe it, but I heard. Let's get going. We need to find the Ancient One, the Feather, and then get the hell out of here."

"I don't understand how it can be one of the Four Horsemen. What's so important on Atlantis that they're willing to hurt, even kill, us? Surely, one of those couldn't have started the earthquake."

"I doubt that, but it just makes our journey more dangerous. You feel good enough to move on and up?"

"Yeah, let's go." I grab Jerome's hand, grateful for his strength and his friendship. I reach for the backpack.

"I've got it, Rosa."

Hand in hand, we start our journey again.

CHAPTER 9

FOUND

We climb, following the contours of the land. There's no real path, just rocks, mud. and ice. Can't remember how many times I've fallen. Once an ice shard ripped a hole in my pants. I'm sweating in all these clothes, and the wind keeps blowing. Probably going to catch pneumonia. That will be hard to explain. Added to all that, my breathing is heavy and fast, like I'm on my last legs. We live in the Mile High City at the foot of the Rocky Mountains and several 14ers! This should be an easy climb. Only it's not.

"Okay, Rosa?" His voice is strained.

"Yes," I croak. At least he's just as out of breath as I am, in spite of his training. Several times I've reached out to Jerome who grabs my hand and pulls me up the steepening slopes.

About halfway up to the ice sheet, we stop for a rest and to get our breathing under control.

"At this rate, Jerome, we'll both have heart attacks before we reach the glacier."

"I thought I was in decent shape."

"You are...just not for climbing up to a glacier. It's not the height, it's the steep slope and the rocks, moss, and ice. With every step I take, I slide back two. Look," I say pointing back the way we came. "It's hard to even find the spot where we started from. It's below and under us! Even the river is almost invisible." I shiver at the memory of crossing that river just a while ago.

"I think we still have a long climb ahead of us. And if we sit on these rocks for much longer, my butt is going to freeze. Everything up here is covered in ice."

I giggle and then cover my mouth with my hand. It'd be too easy to lose control.

"Rosa, look there!" Jerome gets up and walks over to a piece of melting ice, at least that's what it looks like.

"Where?"

He grabs my arm and pulls me to his side. There in the pool of melting ice, amid the dirt and ash, are footprints!

"What..." I utter, bending over to take a closer look.

"Exactly, my thoughts."

"Who? What?'

Another faint laugh reaches us. Its mocking sound sends chills through my body.

"Jerome?"

"Yeah, one of the Horsemen is definitely here." He runs hand through his damp hair, his hat gone by the wayside a while back. "But, surely it can't be John King, right? We left him on Telendos or somewhere over there."

"That's what I thought." Pushing up from the rock

with one hand, I stand on shaky legs. "That leaves three more, though." Softly, but full of evil, the laugh mocks us.

"Yeah, I know."

He kneels down again to study the footprints closer. "These prints are small. They're not even human." He looks behind us.

Blowing snow and fog swirl over the icy hills. I want to tell him that I'm not sure the Horsemen are human, but I keep silent.

He stands up. "We have to go keep going."

I swallow hard. My heart pounds against my chest and the ankh vibrates in time with it. "I know."

"Whatever's up here, we'll face together." He stands beside me, his eyes on the glacier. "We'd best get moving and find that Ancient One." He holds out a hand. "C'mon. We'll travel close from now on."

I grasp his hand and, with another glance at the river, match his steps.

Our climb doesn't get any easier, but we are closer now to the edge of the glacier. Although steeper, we don't have the big rocks and boulders to climb around. The ground is littered with those polished pebbles and small rocks. It doesn't help that moss covers most of those making our footing tricky.

"Rosa, look there. More footprints."

I stop and bend down to see better.

These look the same, small and not human. Almost animal-like. Wait a minute! I push in front of Jerome to get closer. Getting down on my knees, I put my hand on top of a print. "Jerome, could these be a cat's paw prints?"

"Here? No way. What would a cat be doing here? Anyway, I read that cats are considered bad luck in Iceland."

I turn to look at him. "Bad luck?"

"Yep. I read that last night. At least I think it was last night. They're shapeshifters or something like that." He looks beyond me and points. "Come on. Let's see where they lead."

He climbs up another steep slope, knocking down rocks as he tries to find footholds.

I scramble up as best I can, but I'm still sliding two steps back for each one forward. My chest aches. My head's still pounding. My whole body hurts.

"Jerome."

He stops, reaches back, and pulls me up. Linking his arm with mine, we continue to the edge of the actual glacier where the paw prints stop.

"What the..." Jerome says looking around.

"It or whatever couldn't just disappear. There's nothing but solid ice here. Where did it go?"

Nowhere. I'm right here.

I jump and grab Jerome, my head spinning.

"What, Rosa?"

"Whatever it is, just spoke to me!"

"No way."

"Yes. Said it's right here." Frantically I search around. "Do you see anything?"

I sense rather than see Jerome freeze. He's staring

at the glacier's edge. I follow his gaze and drop to the ground scraping my hands as I break my fall.

Sitting on the glacier, almost invisible, is an enormous cat, an enormous white cat with one blue eye and one yellow eye!

CHAPTER 10

AN<IENT ONE

The giant cat stares back at us, each eye seeming to focus on one of us.

The blue eye on Jerome, the yellow one on me.

"What the hell, Rosa!" Jerome says as he helps me up. Not letting go of his hand, I stumble over my next words. "It has to be some kind of genetic disorder, don't you think?"

"Beats me."

I can do that, but it will waste even more time. I've been waiting for you for a long while.

I squeeze his hand so hard, my nails bite into his skin.

"Ow, Rosa!" He pulls his hand away and rubs the red indentations.

"Sorry. The cat says it's been waiting for us."

"You really heard it? Dumb question."

Not bothering to answer, I just nod several times.

"You think this is the Ancient One?"

Rosa, tell Jerome I am known as the Ancient One in this land.

"It says yes. And it knows our names."

"Why am I not surprised?"

There's his sarcastic side again.

Rosa, tell him to place his palm flat on the glacier.

"Why?"

"What, Rosa?"

"The cat says to place your palm flat on the glacier. I don't know why," I say before he can ask.

Jerome glares at the cat before doing as instructed. He flinches at the cold but keeps it there.

You can remove your hand, Jerome.

He jumps back, pulling his hand off the glacier. "Did you hear that, Rosa? Of course, you did."

I nod. "You heard also?"

Shaking his head, he says, "Unreal, but yeah, I did. Just like with the Atlantean Horse. I touch, and I hear."

The cat appears to nod.

"You said you've been waiting for us?" I ask.

I am the Ancient One you seek. My name is Njal.

Looking at his hand still red from the ice, Jerome asks, "How did you do that? And why are your eyes different colors?"

You are full of questions. As to letting you hear me, it was nothing. Part of the magic of this land. As for my eyes, only the gods can answer that.

A stiff wind whips up the snow around us, temporarily blinding us. We both shiver.

When the snow settles, Jerome asks, "Is this weather, this c...cold, common for September?"

Sometimes. But something's disturbed the peace of this land. Something that arrived before you.

"Jerome, the laughter we heard before, do you think...?"

"It shouldn't be possible, but then neither should anything else we've seen."

It came out of the raging surf below Eyjafjallajkull riding a Nykur, a grey Nykur with a red mane and red cheeks.

"From where?" I ask confused

From Eyjafjallajkull, one of our oldest ice coverings.

"I know that name," Jerome says. "I can't begin to pronounce it, but I know it."

Eyjafjallajkull.

"Still can't pronounce it."

"How do you know whatever that is?" I ask, puzzled.

"In science class, we studied geology and volcanic eruptions. This volcano erupted back in 2010."

"But this is a glacier."

"I know, Rosa, but the volcano under the glacier has the same name. The explosion when it erupted sent ash, smoke, and debris up into the skies above Iceland and most of Europe for weeks. Our teacher said that the amount of ash literally turned day into night it was so heavy. Disrupted air traffic and really messed up flying.

"Did people die?"

"No one did. Iceland evacuated them in plenty of time. Think they've had plenty of practice at that. However, the air quality was so bad that it poisoned the water and ruined the grass fields. When people were finally able to move back, most had no place to go back to. So many homes and structures were destroyed."

"Are there volcanoes still erupting today?"

"All the time. Gee, Rosa, you need to follow the news. Iceland's had several in the past few years, but nothing like that Ey... one."

Eyjafjallajokull.

"Nope, still can't say it," he answers shaking his head.

Well, you seem to know more about my home than I thought.

"He knew a lot about Telendos too, where our grandpa lives."

"I like geology. In fact, Rosa, did you know that the most dangerous volcano in the whole world is in our own backyard?" His arms spread out, adding emphasis to his words.

"What?"

"Yes, it's in Yellowstone. They say if that volcano ever blows, half of our country will be wiped out!"

"What?" I say again.

"Yeah, that's what the scientists say, but it's not likely to happen."

"Well, that's a small comfort."

Don't you think we should be talking about the evil that is here now?

"Sorry," I say.

Jerome glares at the cat and asks, "So what is this Nykur? And what riding it?"

The Nykur is a waterhorse.

"Wait," I jump in. "Waterhorses are Kelpies."

In some lands these creatures are known as Kelpies. In Iceland, they are called Nykurs. And here, where horses are considered descendants of the gods, Nylurs are capable of

*both good and evil. Just like the gods. It takes lots of magic
to ride the Nykur.*

"But I read that Kelpies ... Nykur drown those who
ride them."

"Was that in the Horses of the Ancient World book
that Grandpa gave to you?"

"No, in the *Mythology of the Ancient Races.*"

*Yes, Nykurs are an evil horse, a river diver. But they
can be ridden if one is able to put a bridle on them. The
evil one riding the Nykur did that. It took great magic for
a shapeshifter to tame the Nykur and now great evil is
present here.*

"A shapeshifter?" I question.

Yes. Riding the Nykur.

"But, aren't..."

Jerome puts his arm around me and crushes me to
his side. I try again. "But the..." His fingers dig into my
shoulder stopping me.

The cat's eyes shift from one of us to the other,
suspiciously, as if sensing what I was about to say.

"Rosa," Jerome jumps in. "Remember what we
heard earlier?"

Still confused, I answer, "You mean the laughter?"

"Yes," he answers.

 "Wait. You think that the shapeshifter on the Ny..."

Nylur, the cat adds.

"...on the Nylur is one of them?"

"I don't know what to think, Rosa. It makes as much
sense as anything else."

Who are 'they'? What one?

"The man, or shapeshifter, as you called him might

be one of the Four Horsemen," I explain, "of the Apocalypse. From the *Bible*. One rides a white horse and is considered the conqueror or king."

"We ran into him on Telendos, where our grandfather lives," Jerome says.

"Another one rides a black horse and brings famine or eruptions. Still another rides a pale or green horse and brings death."

You said there were four.

"The fourth one rides the red horse. He brings war and blood, probably lots of blood. So, he did get here before us," Jerome says, his body sagging as his words sink in.

The cat cocks its head, as if trying to understand what that means.

"They hunt the Feathers of the Phoenix for their own profit..."

"...and are willing to kill to get them," I finish.

CHAPTER 11

PROPHECY

The Phoenix? The fabled bird that heals all illnesses?

"That's the one," Jerome says.

Why is he here? The Phoenix never lived here.

"No," I say, "but one of its Feathers is here somewhere. That's what we're here for. To find the second Feather. We found the first one on Telendos, although it almost caused the death of Nikos, our grandfather's friend."

The cat's tail twitches, leaving small tuffs of fur on the ice.

"Rosa, how did he get here first? How did he know to even come here?"

"He knows the same prophecy. That's how. That's why King showed up on Telendos."

What is this prophecy?

I looked at Jerome who nods. Then I begin:

"*Ancient Priestesses*

Whispered of the Five Feathers:

One was kept close to the one who survived.

"The one on Telendos," Jerome adds. "We found that one where the Atlantean Horse is.

One was sent north to the Old Gods.

"That's here. Iceland." Jerome ignores my glare.

One was sent into the fires of Hephaestus.

One was sent to the land of the Druids.

One was sent to the land of the Pharaohs.

All to be revealed on the worship Days of the Sun.

"And today's the Autumnal Equinox, a day of Sun worship," Jerome adds.

Whispered of the Four Horsemen who would ride from the edges of the Ancient World seeking the Feathers and the ones holding them. The Four Horsemen who rode in the name of Conquest, War, Famine, and Death. Sometimes aided, and sometimes opposed, by the Four Winds from Aeolus Island: East, West, North, and South.

"I'd say the North Wind is here today," Jerome interrupts again. "And not helping us!"

I glare at him.

"Sorry. Just wanted to add more for its benefit." He points at the cat.

Whispered of how beneath the blazing sun all await the ones who will gather the Feathers of the Phoenix for the rising of Atlantis."

"And that's why we're here. To find you and have you lead us to the second Feather," Jerome said.

"Yes," I add. "We're supposed to follow you under the Norse Star to the past. That's what Mneseus said."

Who's this Mneseus?

"He's the Atlantean that brought us here," Jerome says. "You don't know him?"

Getting nothing but a stare from the cat, Jerome swears under his breath. I punch him in the arm.

"Sorry, Rosa. This is beyond crazy. How are we supposed to find the Feather when Mneseus couldn't tell us who the Ancient One even was? And this cat didn't know about the prophecy or who Mneseus was?"

I have no answer.

The cat's yellow and blue eyes widen to twice their size. Without a word, it stands, turns away from us, and vanishes in the glacier ice.

ᚦᚱ ᚾᚦᛏ ᛚᛑᛋᛇ

The Fair One and her protector know of the prophecy. They also know of my shapeshifters. They may not be dangerous to my land, but may find themselves in great danger.

CHAPTER 12

THE HORSEMAN

Bulked up by a heavy black coat, hood pulled over its head, wearing padded army pants and thick-soled boots, the rider kicks the grey devil horse in the flanks and yanks on the reins flicking the red mane. Beneath them the ground rumbles and shakes. The Nylur hesitates for only a second before plunging into the fast-moving water. Leaning upstream, it traverses the glacier river with its odd running walk. Leaning slightly with the horse, his knees gripping the sides of the creature, the rider fights the awkward gait, not wanting to swim in the icy waters.

Never would he learn to ride these animals that forded rivers on their sides. There had better not be too many more of these. But if there were, he knew he'd ford them. No way he'd lose this Feather to those kids! What he couldn't figure out was how they got the time wrong. Good thing he knew to listen to the North Wind. It brought him to the Nylur. And the Nylur was now bringing him to where he needed to be, whether it wanted to or not. He knew not how everything worked, didn't matter that he didn't understand. What was important was that he was ahead of those two. He figured it out before they did. Imagine thinking that a cat could help them!

A jolt brings him out of his thoughts. The Nylur leaps up the river bank and stops. The ground is silent here. The rider looks around him. Lumps of volcanic rock, some covered in moss, spread out across the land. He sweeps off his hood. For just a moment he stares in amazement at the green and red fingers of light that dance across the sky above him. The air, warmed by the sulfur fumes spewing out of the volcanic vents, speaks volumes to him.

Somehow in crossing the river, the Nylur delivered him to the early years, long before the Saga era, longer even than before the first settlers found their way here. And in some strange way, so had the Phoenix Feather. His eyes sweep over the desolate landscape searching for the entrance. A strange light from above reveals a faint path through the broken land, the Norse light. He doesn't hesitate to follow it, determined to find the Feather first.

It won't be long now. Somewhere in this forgotten past, the Feather waits. Waits for whoever gets there first. Waits for me. I'll get it and be gone before they ever find their way here. Following a cat! That cat will be replaced soon by a shapeshifter. They won't even know they follow a shapeshifter until it's too late. Until I have the Feather!

Evil flows from this one. And Danger. His grasp on the magic of this land is unheard of before.

CHAPTER 13

ALONE...AGAIN

Clutching Jerome's arm, I search the glacier.

"Jerome...?"

He shakes his head as he pries my fingers from his arm. Two steps and he's at the glacier. Climbing up, he stays on his knees, sweeping his hands over the frozen surface.

"Nothing."

I clamber up beside him, turn around in circles scouring the glacier and the ground, shading my eyes from the glare.

"Rosa...Rosa! What are you doing?"

"Looking for the cat, for Njal."

"You're kidding, right?" A smile spreads across his face.

I give him a scalding look.

He waves his hand around. "Looking for a white cat on a glacier? Absolutely crazy!"

He grabs my hand and pulls me down beside him.

"Relax. Just sit and relax."

"And then what, Jerome?"

He shrugs. "We don't have a clue as to where to go.

So, we wait."

"Be nice if someone cut symbols in the ice like the cave on Telendos."

"Yes, it would." He's staring at the ground with that thoughtful look of his. "Do you think we can trust that cat?"

"You mean because Icelandic cats are supposed to be shapeshifters?" I ask.

"Exactly. And the fact that it knew someone, or something, was here before us. Plus, it has different colored eyes! That in itself is a bit disconcerting, don't you think?"

"I agree with all of that. I have heard of cats and dogs with two different color eyes before. Rare, but it happens somehow. But if the cat, Njal, is really the Ancient One, then, yes, I guess we wait."

Jerome picks up a handful of pebbles and tosses them up and down.

"We're in Iceland! Sitting at the edge of a glacier! Nothing around us but ice!" He chuckles softly. "No one will ever believe us."

"I know. I've spent most of my life knowing and hearing things I can't share with anyone." I put my hand on his knee. "At least we're here together."

He puts his hand on top of mine. "Here, here. What's that old saying? All for one and one for all. Right?"

"Yes."

Laughter? Do they not understand the danger they may be in? Surely, they must. If not, they will soon. The Evil grows in my land. I cannot protect them and my land at the same time.

I look off into the distance, to the far reaches of the ice sheet in front of us. "What you said about Grandpa, last night. I've been thinking about that."

"I know. Me too."

"Do you," I hesitate, not sure I can voice what I'm thinking. Not sure if I want to. "Do you think Grandpa plans on...."

"Leaving here if Atlantis really rises?"

"Yes," I whisper, tears filling my eyes. I blink hard.

"I don't know, Rosa. I really don't know."

He puts his arm around my shoulders and draws me close.

"I don't want him to die, Jerome. And that's what would happen, wouldn't it?"

Jerome wipes his eyes and nods slowly. "Yes. Yes, that's what would happen."

He gives me a hug and then takes his hand from my shoulders. He's not an emotional person, but Grandpa has always been there, a constant in our lives. He's our last living grandparent. It will be devastating to lose him. We sit quietly, each lost in our thoughts.

CHAPTER 14

GONE?

You shouldn't be here.

"What the..."

"Bloody hell!" Jerome adds, jumping to his feet.

Behind us on the glacier is Njal.

You shouldn't be here. That which you seek has been gone from here for eons.

"That can't be right," I say.

"We need that Feather," Jerome says.

The one who sent you failed in his mission.

"But the Horseman is here, the one who rides the ... Nylur. Rosa, something's wrong."

"I know."

The Horseman is gone.

"What?" Jerome asks. "Gone?"

"How can he just be gone?"

The cat's front shoulders rise; its blue and yellow eyes narrow.

"Did it just shrug its shoulders?"

I just stare at the cat. Cradling my head in shaking hands, I take a couple of deep breaths, hoping to calm my racing heartbeat.

"What now?" Jerome asks, knowing I don't have an answer.

"And where do *we* go, Jerome? Even more important, where did *he* go?"

Into the past.

"Into the past?" We both echo.

Yes. Beyond the Age of Settlement. Beyond what is known as the Saga Age. Beyond the time of humans in this place.

"What are you talking about?" Jerome exclaims.

"Wait. Remember what Mneseus told us?"

"Yes, follow the Ancient One into the past."

The Past. Beyond the Age of Settlement in 870 when the Vikings came and stayed. But we are much older than people know. Eons older and the old ways still live here. And although the Sagas tell the tales of Settlement, long before the beginning of its time, this island has been inhabited by mystical beings. Trolls, hags, shapeshifters, and other spirits still roam this land. Their stories are woven into our history. People feared these beings who could appear at first benevolent and then turn evil and attack. Many Icelanders still believe in and talk to elves.

"No way," Jerome says. "Elves? Trolls? Hags? Those belong in fairy tales. It's like saying Santa Claus and the Easter Bunny are real. Children believe in those, but not adults. We certainly don't."

We'll see.

Once again, the cat disappears into the glacier ice.

ᚷᚻᚤᛉ

The Protector shows his foolishness. The Fair One needs to take care. No one mocks the Ancient Ones.

CHAPTER 15

ANCIENT PATHS

"Well, he's left again. Now what, Rosa?" Jerome sounds more than a little annoyed. He shakes his head and rolls his eyes.

"I'm not sure." Boy, I've said that a few times.

"Maybe the *cat* knows, if he comes back that is." Okay, more than a little annoyed. He can get this way with me sometimes.

"Well," I say, shrugging my shoulders, "it's worth a shot."

He glares at me, and then his face softens.

"I'm sorry, Rosa. It's … it's just so unreal." He shakes his head. Water droplets fall on his shoulders. Jerome's sigh echoes my own despair. "Elves? Shapeshifters? What's next? The Boogie Man? I thought Mneseus knew what he was doing."

"Maybe he didn't understand. Either way, we need to figure out how to get to, and then past, the settlement/saga ages," I say.

"Too bad we've no way to contact him. Bet he could get us there quickly."

I grab my stomach, glad to a small degree that I

don't have to go through a Time Wrap again so soon.

I can show you the way, if you want.

"Geez! Can you not creep up on us like that?" Jerome says, bumping into me and glaring at the cat.

A little nervous, are we?

"You bet we are. And why should we trust you to do what Mneseus couldn't?"

You could just stay here. Let that Horseman get your precious Feather.

Jerome clinches his fists. His body stiffens.

I jump into the conversation.

"Let's calm down just a bit," I say to both of them. I look directly at the cat. "Can do you that? Get us to where we need to go?"

"Rosa!" Jerome says, taking a step toward the cat.

My hand on his arm stops any further progress or words.

"Well, can you?"

Yes. I know the old ways. There are paths back to the early days of this land. Paths that few know. Paths not traveled anymore except by old ones, magical ones.

Jerome takes my hand off his arm and pulls me away from Njal.

"Rosa," he whispers. "I don't like this. How do we know we can even trust this...this shapeshifter?"

"We don't have any other choice if we want to get the Feather first. The Horseman is out there right now looking for the Feather," I pause, unsure if I should say what I'm thinking. "Remember what Grandpa told us that night?"

"Not all of it."

"About the magic. He said there's a lot of magic in the world, but most choose not to believe because life is easier that way. But we need to believe, Jerome, if we're going to find the Feather first."

Jerome stands silently, and then finally nods. We both turn to Njal.

"Okay," he says. "How do we do this?"

Follow me.

"Yeah, right. Follow the cat!"

I punch his arm and follow the cat. He follows, although reluctantly.

ᚠᚼᛁᛚᚼᛘ

Interesting that someone called Grandpa makes them believe in our magic.

CHAPTER 16

EVIL DESCENDS

All around the valley floor, fissures and rifts break up what might have been a smooth surface. Peppered with volcanic lava rocks, snow still sits as if frozen in time on mossy ground. Winter often comes in early September in these extreme northern latitudes. Across the valley lies a huge cold lake fed only by glaciers. Several of the fissures and rifts are filled with the lake water.

At the edge of one fissure stands a monstrous troll. Dark brown fur frames its face and encircles its pointed ears. A black coat and pants stretch across the large body, seams close to bursting in several places. Kneeling down, it places furry hands on the sides of the earth and peers down into the darkness. Squinting, it tries to decipher the distance to the bottom. Jagged rocks line the way down. Turning its head, the troll listens intently, hearing the faint lapping of water.

"This is the place. The old stories told of this place where East once met West. Where every day, the two move further apart. One day some of those countries will simply cease to exist. One day only islands will be afloat. That day, Atlantis will be our new home. And its wealth will let us dominate all of this world and those who think it is their land."

His crooked smile reveals broken teeth with bits of stems and grasses caught in the empty spaces between them. Standing up, the troll turns its head all the way around. Seeing nothing moving on the lava fields, it bends down and scratches between its fur-covered toes, pulling out pieces of volcanic rock and moss stuck there.

Tethered away from the fissure, the Nylur watches, its red mane shining against the grey body. From time to time, it ducks its head and nibbles at the moss-covered rocks. Thick-soled boots still dripping water stand close by.

"Keep a look out," the troll growls. "I shouldn't be long."

He lowers himself into the fissure, using the rocks on the sides to make his way down into the darkness. The Nylur watches until the troll disappears down into the broken earth. Then it goes back to nibbling the sparse grass.

↑ᚸᚴᛈᛁᛉᛏᚴᚼ

So, he reveals the real reason he and his kind are after the Feathers.

CHAPTER 17

THE CHOSEN ONES

Njal leads us along the edge of the glacier. We follow silently. Jerome's constantly looking around. Me, my head's bobbing between the ground and our surroundings. The moss-covered rocks are tricky to traverse. The last thing I want to do is fall and twist an ankle or worse.

Other than the moss, no other vegetation grows here. No trees. No bushes. Nothing. And as for other living creatures: we are it.

Jerome punches me in the arm. "Rosa, look!"

"What?" Then it hits me. "What's that smell?"

"It's what I wanted you to see. That smell's coming from up ahead. See all the steam rising out of the ground?"

Njal has stopped to see what we're doing.

We need to move along.

"What is this place? What's happened to the glacier?' I ask.

In your time, this is called Namafjall, a geothermal field.

We've moved along an ancient path. One that is not seen by others. One only those who have been here forever know.

"That's crazy," Jerome says.

Maybe in your world, but not in mine.

"It's like stepping into a room full of rotten eggs." I plug my nose and try to breathe through my mouth. Jerome's doing the same.

Steaming hot pools of water are everywhere. Heat radiates all around us. In awe, we stare at this strange landscape.

"It's like something out of Jules Verne's *Journey to the Center of the Earth.*"

"Or like being on the surface of the moon," Jerome adds.

I move closer to a steaming pool, my hand outstretched. Jerome pulls my arm back.

"You crazy, Rosa? That's scalding water. Look how it's burnt the dirt and bleached some places white."

Come, we must find the path below.

"Below?" We both echo.

Yes. To reach the place of the Feather, we must abandon this world and travel through the ages underneath. If you would have looked up, you would have seen that we have been following the Norse Star. See?

We both look up and exclaim. "Wow!"

Racing across the night sky. Wait a darn minute! When did night happen?

"Jerome, it's night up there, but not here."

"I know. I don't know what's happened."

The Norse Star shines in the dark sky to lead travelers.

And there, racing across the night sky are brilliant red, green, and white plumes.

"It's the Northern Lights, Rosa!"

"Wow!" I utter. Looking in front of us, daylight shines bright. "How?"

It's the power of the Norse Star. Not all can see, only the chosen ones.

"And we're the chosen ones?" Jerome asks, again with a bit of sarcasm.

Apparently so. Come.

With that, Njal leads us through the field of bubbling water holes and smoking stacks of volcanic rocks. We follow hesitantly, cautiously. If we step wrong, we'll find ourselves immersed in boiling liquid. That wouldn't be fun. I take a shallow breath and start choking. My word, I thought the bat guano in the cave smelled bad! I may never eat another egg again! This smell's so overwhelming, if it doesn't let up, I'm going to puke right here.

Njal stops at one of the stacks and waits. As we get closer, the cat shimmers for just a moment and seems to grow five times its size. We freeze.

"What the....?' Jerome whispers.

A hole opens up next to the smoking stack of volcanic rocks. Njal returns to his normal size and, with a backward glance at us, disappears down the hole.

Moving closer, we find ourselves staring down into a crevice. Jagged rocks line the sides. A broken path leads down into the earth. Down into a black abyss.

"Njal?"

Come.

Although we still see his outline, his voice reaches up as if he's miles below. *This is the path.*

We look at each other, both unsure.

Come. It won't be open for long. Njal jumps further down to a ledge. He shimmers once again, growing in size. A sound like a wounded meow reaches us.

We gasp as he returns back to normal.

He jumps deeper into the crevice. Come. His voice almost a whisper now. His body disappearing in the shadows.

"What the devil, Jerome?" I whisper.

"He just might be, but we have no choice. Stick close to me."

ᚠᚩᚦᚾᛋᚾ

I'm afraid these two might be too trusting.

CHAPTER 18

DEEP DOWN

Jerome goes first. I follow so close I'm almost on top of him.

The crevice is narrow, steep, and dark. We feel our way down carefully holding onto the rough volcanic rocks on either side. Definitely not the same volcanic rocks you would find in a rock shop or the pebbles we found on the shore. No polishing of these. They have just been dropped here from an eruption. As we continue down, the rocks grow cold and wet.

We keep climbing down, the crevice narrowing so much at times that we have to squeeze through sideways.

"Crap. Rosa, watch out. The sides narrow more. Just smacked my arm on a sharp edge. Probably tore my coat."

I reach out and tap Jerome on the shoulder. He stops and turns around.

"Are we crazy?" I whisper.

"Probably, but I don't know what else to do."

"Mneseus did send us to him, at least I think so."

"After that little stunt at the opening, I'm not so sure

this is the same Njal." He takes a breath.

"You mean that shimmering or whatever that was?"

"Yes. Something definitely happened up there."

"You think a shapeshifter is leading us now?"

"I have no idea. Keep alert. We may be getting in deeper than we know."

Leave it to Jerome to use a pun!

The path has become so steep that the way forward descends into a black hole.

"Can you see the cat or whatever we've followed down here?" I whisper in his ear.

"No, but I think the path is getting flatter."

Indeed, we now appear to be traveling in a straight line. Eerily, so like Verne's story.

"How long have we been in here?"

"I don't know, Rosa. I haven't been able to see my watch since we started down. Could be an hour or several."

"Njal?" I call out.

Time here is not your time. We are traveling into the past not in today.

"I hate to ask this, but how is this possible?" Jerome whispers to me.

I shrug and have no answer.

We are almost there.

"Almost where?" I utter, expecting no answer.

"More important, what are we following?"

ᛏᛊᛊᚦ ᛏᚻᚲᚲᚾ

What indeed, travelers. Something is not right with this cat. This is why we have never welcomed them in our land. It has been whispered that cats are shapeshifters. That may be true with this one. Somehow the evil one has been given the power to call and command this cat.

CHAPTER 19

DANGER

"Any idea what direction we're going in?"

"None. This is worse than that cave on Telendos," Jerome says.

Memories of that darkness, the odious smell of bat guano, the overwhelming sense of being followed, and the explosion that came soon after starts my body shaking.

"Jerome, what if … what if this time instead of being followed, we're being led?" My voice trembles.

Jerome shakes his head.

The darkness closes in on us. Glancing back, I see no light of any kind. Ahead, nothing but blackness. My heart's pounding. This is insane. What are we thinking? I reach for Jerome's arm but find nothing.

Panicking, I push forward determined to find him before he gets too far ahead. That's when it happens. The ground beneath my feet shakes. Shards of rock fall from above. Brushing those out of my hair, I open my mouth to scream for Jerome.

A hand clamps down on my lips. I struggle, flaying out with clinched fists. Another hand pushes me against the rock wall, into the ragged side. Warm breath fans across my face. I continue to fight. Then...

"Rosa, stop it. It's me. Jerome."

My body goes limp. Jerome takes his hand from my mouth and eases up. I suck in the damp, horrid air, not even noticing the rotten egg smell at first. Then I start gagging.

"What ... what just happened? Where were you?" I'm angry and relieved at the same time.

"Just ahead. You stopped. I turned around, and you were gone," he said somewhat accusingly.

"Sorry. The darkness got to me when you mentioned the cave on Telendos." I take another deep breath. "Where's the cat?"

"I ... don't ... know."

"Was that an earthquake?"

"I'd bet on it."

"Where's the cat?"

"Really? How should I know? Somewhere ahead of us would be my guess."

"Sorry. Shouldn't we go on?"

He reaches down and pulls a flashlight out of his coat pocket.

"Didn't want to be unprepared. And it's a good thing." He points the light above and behind us.

I gasp. Huge boulders block our path out.

"Okay, that answers my question. Might as well see if Njal is still ahead of us."

"Right. Or if he's led us down a dead end." He shines the light down ahead of us. "Stay here. I'll go on ahead and then light your way."

I watch as he makes his way down through the narrow corridor. *Where is that cat? Or whatever we've followed."* I shiver at the thought that we've been tricked. Then the light shines on my legs. Relieved, I make my way down testing, each foothold to be sure it's stable.

Jerome's waiting, probably a bit impatient.

"Any sign of the cat?' I ask.

"No."

Just then a voice calls out to us.

About time. Let's keep moving. We're almost there.

"And just where is that?" I ask.

The past. Where the Feather should be.

↑ᚻᚼᚷᛁR

The earth shakes, trying to expel the evil.

CHAPTER 20

LEGEND

The sound of roaring water grows until it's impossible to even hear my thoughts. Up ahead a sliver of light appears. Our path has widened enough that we are walking side by side. We each trail a hand along the sides. How strange there are no carved images on these walls. Jerome's turned off the flashlight.

We've only heard Njal, but it would be comforting to see him… I think.

At the end of the underground path, we both stop, our mouths wide open. The roaring water pours down as if from the sky. Somehow we've ended up behind the waterfall!

"What in the world, Rosa?" He asks, screaming in my ear.

"Amazing!" I yell back at him.

Stepping carefully out of the darkness, we find ourselves in a downpour. Neither of us utters a word. It only takes a couple of minutes for the mist to cover our clothes. Still frozen, we just stand and stare at the sight before us.

How long are you going to stand there?

"W...what?" I stutter.

Jerome takes my hand and pulls me onto the ledge.

"Rosa! Look at this!"

Beyond the veil of pouring water is a fast running river. Beyond that, the mist rises into the air. Tumbling water splashes down, sending shoots of moisture onto the ledge beneath us and the surrounding land.

"There," Jerome points.

Njal waits past the waterfall, further along the ledge.

OMG! This desolate land around us is filled with more rocks and moss.

By the time we reach Njal, we are both soaked, and water is running off us as if we were the mountain!

"Just where are we?" Jerome asks.

Njal points to the river flowing from the waterfall. *That is the River Skoga. It flows from forests deep within the island. This is its last fall before it empties into the sea, just over there.*

Beyond where he is pointing, the land disappears. Spreading out from there is water, nothing else. Just water.

"Jerome, would that be..."

"Yeah, that's the Atlantic Ocean. Wow, what a sight!"

"I hope we don't have to go very much further. I don't want to swim today."

"As if we could get any wetter!"

This is the end of the island. In your time, frequent volcanic eruptions have pushed the edge further out.

"You mean, this doesn't look like this now?" Jerome asks.

No. In your time, the river flows a great distance before finding the sea. Much has changed from this time to your time. Much.

While I'm interested, I'm more concerned with finding the Feather. I'm sure the day is passing. I nudge Jerome.

"Right. Njal, what do we do here?"

Long before the legend of Prasl Porolfsson started, it is told that a strange object floated down from the Heavens seeking protection. The Spirits of this land welcomed it and hid it in the River Skoga.

"Wait," I interrupt. "I'm guessing that the object was the Feather of the Phoenix, but..."

"Hold up! Just who or what is Pras Porolson?" Jermone's just about ready to explode.

Prasl Por-olf-sson. Njal slowly pronounces the name for us.

Jerome rolls his eyes. I squeeze his arm to prevent another outburst. We need Njal. Jerome is not a patient person. The Atlantean Horse knows, and Njal is learning fast.

It is told that Prasl was the first Viking to settle here around the year 900.

"But that's long after the Feather would have landed here." Great, now I'm getting impatient. This is close to not making any sense.

True. But that is how legends come about. Some truth, some untruth.

Jerome rolls his eyes. "Go on, please." That sarcastic voice again.

Njal stares at him, then continues. *Legend says that*

Prasl brought with him a chest filled with gold and riches. He didn't want anyone to steal this, so he hid the chest beneath the last falls of the River Skoga. In your time, this is known as Skogafoss

We look at each other and then at the power of the falls.

"Are you telling us that the Feather is buried in a chest that was hidden in the river eons after it arrived here?" Jerome's skepticism is evident, and his voice is getting louder.

"How in the world..."

You must let me finish to understand.

Jerome waves his hand for Njal to continue.

The island Spirits kept the Feather hidden as promised. But it is not as legend says, hidden in Prasl's chest. That was supposedly found centuries later and revealed to be empty. Instead, the Feather, when it first arrived, was hidden in a small break in the rocks beneath the falls.

"So why the story of Prasl?" I ask.

Because some people believe that the chest is still there and contains a hidden treasure. Maybe your Horseman does also.

"Rosa, the Feather is still in the rocks, just like in Telendos."

I picture the hole in the cave wall on Telendos and nod.

"So," Jerome continues, "somehow we are here to find the crack or whatever in the rocks beneath the falls to find the Feather? That's insane!"

"Wait..."

"No, Rosa. How are we supposed to find this ... this

crack? The water will beat us senseless. Just look at how hard and fast it's coming!"

Sadly, I have to agree.

Njal shimmers and grows twice his size. We both jump!

STOP! You do not let me finish!

ᛗᛉᚷᛉᛏᛏ

Something is definitely not right with this cat!

CHAPTER 21

LEGEND OR DECEIT

"Sorry," I murmur.

Jerome mutters under his breath.

It is said that because of the volcanoes, the Spirits became worried that the Feather would be buried forever, so they moved it.

I don't know what I look like, but Jerome's mouth is open, and his eyes are straight up to the heavens.

"Okay," Jerome starts. "Let me see if I know what you're trying to tell us: The Feather was put in the rocks when it first came. Right?"

He waits for Njal's nod.

Boy, we're really getting in deep. Now I see the cat nodding. I put my head in my hands hoping to maintain my sanity.

"Then this Prasl dude came and hid a chest of gold and riches here in the river beneath the falls."

He waits again. Njal nods.

"And, when the chest was found later, it was empty. But volcanic eruptions made this river unstable. So, you follow me, Rosa?"

I nod, but don't lift my head.

"It, the Spirits, then determined that the Feather might be lost forever, so they moved it to the chest. Considering that since the chest had already been found empty, no one would bother it again. Am I right?"

Njal nods. I don't do anything.

"So," he continues in that skeptical voice, "the Feather is still here, in the river, but in the chest."

So the legend says.

"Jerome, my brain's going to explode!"

"I know, but wait just a minute."

He moves closer to Njal, who holds his ground

"You just said a minute ago that legends are part truth, part untruth."

The two just stare at each other.

OMG, I'm going crazy! This is worse than trying to figure out what was missing on the walls of Tut's tomb!

ᚁᛚᚠᛋᛁᛗ

So how does the cat know all this? And why is it the first time I've heard of this? I suspect the cat is not telling the whole truth.

CHAPTER 22

EVIL FIRST!

Lumbering along underground through the fissure, the troll curses as his foot hits another rock jutting out of the ground. Nothing is smooth here in the rift that separates East and West. Only jagged edges of granite, once whole, remain. That and the cries. Millenniums of wounded cries being torn apart echo off the walls. But these fall on deaf ears. The troll doesn't listen, isn't interested. Only one thing fills his mind: his dogged determination not to fail as King did. "I Will Not Fail," he screams.

His voice drowns out the echoing cries. And, then, an upheaval in the land collapses the path behind him. Dust and rocks fall around him. He swats at those as one would a fly. All to no avail. Shaking his hairy head, he wipes the dust from his eyes. "Only one way out now. Possibly for all of us!"

Determined not to fail, he treks on, over rocks, moss, and small pools of heated lava. From time to time, he stops to wipe the sweat from his hairy head. The sulfuric gases he breathes in faze him very little. The only thing that matters is to get there first. To get to the Feather first!

CHAPTER 23

SURPRISE!

"This is stupid. Either you know where the Feather is, or you don't! Which is it, Cat?"

Jerome's really losing it.

Njal shimmers again. The ground shakes beneath us. Huge rocks crash down into the pool.

"Rosa, Move!"

Jerome grabs my hand, or maybe I grab his. Running and dodging debris, we jump over the moss-covered rocks to reach a safe distance from the falling boulders. I chance a look back, but Njal has disappeared!

Crouching on the ground, we cover our heads as shards of rock, pumice, and ice rain down. I look back for Njal. Still not there.

"Jerome, he's gone!"

"What?"

"Njal, he's gone!"

In spite of the earthly missiles still pelting us, he jumps up. Turning around he looks for himself.

"Great. Just Great!"

Something by the falls catches my eye. I walk over for a closer look.

"Be careful, Rosa."

I reply with a wave of my hand, my focus on my discovery. In the middle of the pool of water, just beyond the crashing waterfall, is a whirlpool!

"Jerome, come here. Take a look at this!" I yell to be heard.

Water is swirling around so fast it's creating a funnel that disappears into the earth below. As we watch, the top of the funnel expands outward, but the hole at the bottom keeps going down. Then a belching sound explodes into the air, and the water stops moving. I mean it comes to a complete standstill!

"What now?" Jerome says in my ear. He runs a hand through his red hair showering me with cold water.

I can't even respond. Never have I... we... encountered such phenomenal happenings!

Our eyes stay glued to the hole.

A shadow appears in the hole, a small dark spot gradually gaining in size.

Dumbfounded, we watch unable to move or speak.

As a shape emerges, I gasp!

"What the hell, Rosa?"

Two white ears appear from the shadow. One is bent.

Next comes a cat face with one blue eye and one yellow eye! A stripe of black extends across the face.

Once even with the ground, the cat jumps out of the hole, dripping wet and covered in black stripes like zebra.

"Njal?" We both utter.

Yes. Finally, it's me.

Finally? We have no words, too stunned and confused.

Come, follow me. We have much to talk about.

We follow obediently, like zombies being summoned by their master.

ᚲᛏᚱᚦᚱᛁᚲᛉ

Maybe now the truth will come out. Out of a cat's mouth?

CHAPTER 24

DECEIT REVEALED

Njal leads us away from the falls and the water. He settles down on a small patch of moss surrounded by rocks.

Jerome glances at me, his eyebrows raised. I shrug my shoulders. Picking a fairly flat rock, I sit down. Jerome does the same. Silently, we wait for Njal to explain.

By now, you should know that the creature which led you here wasn't me.

"What?" We both blurt out.

Njal's head is bobbing up and down. The black stripes across his body ripple like waves in the ocean.

"How is that even possible?" Jerome asks.

I told you.

Jerome interrupts, "You or that … that, whatever that was?"

Njal stares, his two eyes deepen in color..

Me. Things are possible here in this ancient world that aren't in your world.

"Njal?" Me this time. "We are a little..."

"More than a little."

I step on Jerome's foot. "Would you tell us what's going on? Please."

Yes, but you must quit interrupting. We are running short of time.

Njal glares as Jerome opens and then closes his mouth.

Several of the inhabitants of this land are older than you, or anyone, knows. Magic exists here as it has for eons. Even in your time, some of that magic still works as it always has. When you first found me, you were hesitant to trust me.

I start to say something, but just as quickly stop.

I heard your words about shapeshifters and about cats. We were trusted once, but then an evil came over the land and changed many things. We became different than we were. Many tales were told of how we changed shapes and brought the evil to the settlers coming here.

He stops and, if it's possible, seems to bow his head for a brief second.

Glancing at Jerome, I see the skepticism on his face. Me too, if I'm truthful.

Then, not long ago in your time, evil descended again on our land.

"The Nylur," I say.

Yes, but more than that. Nylurs have always been here. What came gave the Nylur greater power. A human-like creature arrived.

"The Horseman riding the horse with the red mane and cheeks," Jerome adds.

Yes. Little did we know then the danger growing in our land.

"We?" Jerome again.

Yes, I am not the only possessor of magic. We have protectors who watch over all of our land. When I led you to the path into the ancient land, I was set upon by another, an evil shapeshifter. It tried to invade my body at the smoking cairns, but I resisted.

"The shimmer?" I ask.

Yes. I threw it off, but then down in the earth, it attacked again.

"The earthquakes and the falling boulders." Jerome adds.

Yes. I was not strong enough to fight it off again. The shapeshifter took over my body. I could only wait until my strength returned.

"In the meantime, we were being led by a ... a whatever. One that didn't want us to succeed." Jerome's mounting anger is so evident.

"But why did it lead us to Skogafoss? To the Feather?"
It didn't.

"What?" We are both so confused.

It didn't lead you to Skogafoss. It led you to Seljalandsfoss. That's why you were able to enter through the falls. Skogafoss' power would have crushed you. It wasn't time yet for you to disappear forever. Njal stops and waits. His eyes move from one of us to the other. Waiting.

"But then..." I start.

"We're at the wrong place," Jerome says. He lowers his head into his hands. "We're at the wrong place," he repeats. No anger this time, just unbearable dejection.

"He was giving the Horseman time to find the Feather," I add, the despair in my voice overwhelms even me.

Njal nods.

Jerome raises his head and looks straight into Njal's eyes. "Can you take us to this Skogafoss?"

Njal nods.

"Then let's go. We may still get there in time!" He stands up, grabs my hand, and pulls me up.

"Yes! Let's go."

CHAPTER 25

ᚳᛚᛟᛋᛂᚱ CLOSER

First, hairy ears appear out of the earth. Then comes the head and body of the troll. Although seemingly impossible, he appears to have grown taller while traveling through the earth.

The roaring of the waterfall fills the air, and the glacier river feeding it stretches across the plateau. Trotting over to the water's edge, he pauses. Turning his head completely around, he surveils the area.

"That cat did the job required of it. I've beat those two here!"

Following the water, he comes to the cliff edge. Here the roar of the falls is even more deafening. This close, the wind blows sheets of icy water all around the troll and threatens to push him over the top.

"Είναι κρύο (It's cold)," he mutters shivering. "Boreas' breath is strong here. Time to get to the bottom and search for the Feather. I can feel its presence!" Turning his back on the wind and water, he finds a path down the side to the bottom.

Still pelted by the freezing spray, he sticks one foot

in the icy pool and jerks it out. His brown fur ripples with the shakes.

Slowly a grin spreads across the hairy face. With a shout of pure evil joy, the troll dives into the deep pool underneath the falls, obvious to the dangers, the ice-cold waters, and the power of the waters raining down.

Far above, a shadow passes overhead.

CHAPTER 26

WHAT NOW?

"So, how do we get to this Skogafoss?" I ask.

"Above ground, I hope," Jerome adds.

Yes. The shapeshifter should be too weak, but I don't want to use the ancient cairn path. We go over a path traveled by elves and others. It's what we call a sacred path. No evil may pass.

"Why didn't we do that before?" Jerome's voice carries an accusing tone.

To get here, the ancient cairns had to be used. Enough questions. We must move fast. I fear for your Feather and my land. Njal dashes off away from us.

"Ready for a race, Rosa?"

I nod. "Let's go before he gets too far ahead.

If you've ever tried to race or catch a cat, then you know that what we've ahead of us isn't going to be easy!

CHAPTER 27

DID HE?

A brown hairy head pops out of the water several yards beyond the cliff. The force of the falls has driven him further downstream. An angry woeful cry erupts from the troll. Water still pelts its head and shoulders. The creature struggles to reach the shore. Raising a fist in the air, he shrieks.

"I will find the Feather. I will."

Turning around, the troll runs back toward the waterfall. Beaten back by the water's powerful force, he bellows and then jumps into the river. With a desperate leap, he plunges into the powerful cascade. His leap is so powerful that rocks resting on the cliff's edge shudder violently before plummeting down, barely missing him.

After several minutes, longer than humans could last under water, his head once again appears from under the water. Oblivious to the pounding spray, his raised arms holding the prize, he fights the current and reaches the shore. Wrapping his arms around his body, he starts back up the rocky mountainside. At the top, he takes one final look down. Moving back from the river and the cliff edge, he sits down on the rocky ground and waits.

All the while a shadow circles overhead.

CHAPTER 28

RA(ING

The sacred path is not smooth. Nothing is on this volcanic island. We have jumped over boulders, slipped on moss-covered stones, and tripped our way up and down the uneven land in our attempt to keep Njal in sight. Three times he's paused and waited until we got close, then takes off again. Just like that pet cat who thinks that the chase is a game.

The ocean is still on our right, and the cliffs tower above us on the left. A roaring sounds in the distance. Maybe the waterfall. Maybe something more sinister.

Another cat pause. Get the double meaning?

I reach for Jerome and groan. I'm breathing so hard I can't even utter a word. One look at me, and he stops. Nice to see he's breathing almost as hard as I am.

With hands on my thighs, I gulp in air.

"If ... it's ... much ... further ... I'm ... not ... sure ... I ... can ... make ... it."

"I ... know ... the ... feeling." Jerome takes a deep breath. He's in better shape, but not by much. "We ... have ... to ... make ... it ... though. There's not much of the day left."

The sun has already started its short journey into the ocean. Night will soon fall.

We both take off again, still fighting for each breath. The closeness of day's end spurs us on. After what seems like another eternity, we see Njal ahead waiting for us.

"Are ... we ... there?" I ask, gasping.

The roaring now fills our ears.

Just up this hill and around that cairn is Skogafoss.

One last climb. The cairn is one of the largest we've seen. From here it looks to be taller than either of us. Suddenly the ground shifts again. Not once, but several times. And hard enough to move boulders. Jerome and I both fall, as we were barely standing as it was.

Ahead of us, the cliffs come alive. Rocks fall, crashing all around. I look for Njal. He's disappeared again!

"Where'd Njal go?"

CHAPTER 29

DANGER DRAWS CLOSER

"Hopefully, not down the cairn again," Jerome yells over the roaring. "Not sure if that's the waterfall roaring or the earth protesting."

Yes.

He speaks from behind us. And although we should be used to his sudden appearances, we both jump.

What you hear is both of those, Jerome. The earth is both angry and afraid. The danger brought here has awakened the protective spirits of this land. If the shaking of the earth doesn't get rid of that evil, then the spirits will bring forth the fire.

"You mean a volcano?" I ask with a shaky voice.

He nods and gives each of us a thorough look over. *"The evil presence is strong here. We must hurry."* He turns and quickens his pace.

Jerome turns to me. "You don't sense anything?"

My hand is throbbing. When I open my fist, the burn spot on my palm from the ankh is bright red. I show Jerome

"Right. We *had* better hurry."

At the top of the hill, we stop, not just because we're both out of breath. No. It is the scene before us that stops us in our tracks.

"OMG!"

I told you the power of Skogafoss would have destroyed you if the shapeshifter had really brought you here.

Ahead a river of water pours over the cliff edge plunging down into a turbulent pool of water. From there, the water turns into a river again and races through a field of tall grasses and moss winding its way to the ocean beyond.

"I've never..."

"Me either, Jerome."

"Where's that cat now?"

We both scour the edge of the pool.

"There!" Jerome yells, pointing to a small shape, tiny at least from this distance, beside the river below.

Slipping and sliding, we make our way down beside him. The roaring of Skogafoss is deafening. And even though we're a long way from the falls, it's not long before we're soaked again. Water sprays everywhere... the shore, the rocks, the grass. Even Njal's fur is soaked, and streams of water run down cleansing his white fur, wiping away the zebra stripes, the visual signs of the shapeshifter's hold on him.

Looking up, only the water is visible against a darkening sky. Day's end is near. And yet, the brightness of the Norse Star lights up the sky.

"What now?" Jerome asks.

Now one of you must go into the pool to find Prasl's chest.

I kneel down and stick my hand into the water. Quickly I pull it out, shaking the water off. "It's freezing!"

Jerome tests it. "Crap. That's beyond cold!"

Njal watches us, amused, I guess.

Well, who will it be?

Embarrassed, I look at the water and then at Jerome. I absolutely abhor cold water. It takes me forever to get into a swimming pool if the water isn't like bath water. And Jerome knows that. He always heads straight for the diving board first, whooping as he dives in.

He puts his arm around my shoulders, giving me a brotherly hug and that lopsided smile.

"I've got this, Rosa."

"I'm so sorry."

"Don't be. I'll get the chest, bring it up. You can open it get, the Feather, and put it in the pouch." Shrugging out of the backpack, he gives my shoulders a quick squeeze.

"You'll freeze when you get out."

"No. Once we have the Feather, Mneseus will come. I'll be fine."

CHAPTER 30

THE PRIZE

Jerome stops at the river's edge. *I've got this. For* Rosa, *the Atlantean Horse, and ... Grandpa.*

Boots off, he sticks a toe in and quickly pulls it out.

"You okay doing this?"

No time for hesitation. He must go.

Jerome nods and walks further into the water, ignoring the cold as it seeps up his clothes and body. Taking a deep breath, he lowers his body up to the shoulders. Pushing toward the middle of the pool, he does his best to ignore the cascade of water from the falls.

The water isn't any deeper than his shoulders. Doggedly he moves forward, eyes on the water, searching for the chest or a shadow. Instead of picking his feet up, he shuffles along the bottom flinching with each scrape and cut from the volcanic rocks.

I watch him, my body shaking with him like I'm in the frigid water.

Halfway back to the cliff, he stumbles. I cry out but hurriedly put my fist in my mouth so he doesn't hear me. He catches his balance. Leaning down, his hands search the icy waters for the object.

Be the chest.

I watch closely, my hands still over my mouth.

Njal watches also, but a faint sound reaches his ears. A huge splash not far from Jerome makes all three of us jump. Three sets of eyes shoot up to the top of the cliff.

Beneath our feet, the earth trembles.

"Njal?" I ask.

It's a small quake miles away. Not here.

"But Jerome..."

Needs to hurry. Another quake could dislodge more boulders.

"Jerome, it was a small earthquake," I yell so he hears me over the roar of the water. "Njal says to hurry before another makes more boulders fall."

"Trying, but my foot's hit something solid here." He bends down again; his hands frantically searching.

There, it's something, maybe the chest. His fingers, nearly frozen, explore the object, the rectangle object, the chest!

"Think I've found it!" Reaching down with both hands, he traces the shape. Carvings cover all sides and the top. "This is it!" Knees bent, he bends further down into the water. *Got to be some kind of handle here. Yes!* "Rosa, it's here. It's heavy but I think I can drag it over to shallower water."

Daring not to hope too much, I rush to the riverbank opposite where Jerome is. "Here, drag it here, and I can help."

Jerome nods, using all of his strength to pull and push the chest.

Njal hasn't moved. He watches intently, but not the two of us. His eyes scan the rock face and the cliff edge above. *Something is not right*, he whispers.

Jerome tugs on the handle. Without warning, it gives way, and he falls face first into the water.

I scream and plunge in, ignoring the icy water. I grab his arm and help him push himself up. "Jerome, are you hurt?"

He shivers. "Just my pride. Should never have tried to pull it." He holds up the handle still clutched in his fist. "But, now, you're all wet too."

Looking down, I see the water dripping down my clothes. I shake just like a dog trying to get rid of the moisture and the cold. "I am. And this water is freezing! Let's try to lift and carry the rest of the way."

We lift the chest just enough to get our hands underneath and move carefully toward the shore.

Njal isn't watching us. His eyes are scanning the cliffs above us.

Hurry, he calls. *Danger is near.*

Glaring at him, we give the chest a final push onto the black pebbles that line the shore. We're both shaking uncontrollably. Jerome pulls the broken handle out of his coat pocket, setting it beside the chest. It's an old chest. The color may have been bright one day; now it just looks like water-soaked wood. The strange carvings are nearly invisible. Only faint lines and half circles still exist.

He grabs a good-sized rock and holds it out to me. "Here, open it, Rosa."

CHAPTER 31

NO!

I take the rock from his hand. Holding my breath, I slowly breathe out trying to calm my racing heart. Awkwardly, I smash the rock into the lock, breaking it. Looking at Jerome, we both nod. Cautiously I lift the chest's lid, my hands shaking uncontrollably.

Once open, I just stare. Stunned, I can't say a word and don't believe my eyes. Then reality kicks me in the stomach. Tears race down my cheeks. Jerome cusses and not under his breath.

"What the hell, Rosa!"

"It's empty! But it can't be. Not after coming this far! It can't be!"

Njal quits staring at the cliff top and comes for a look in the chest. *We are too late.*

"How could we be too late? How could it not be here?" I'm screaming now from frustration, anger, and cold.

Roaring laughter sounds out over the rushing falls.

As one, we all look up.

CHAPTER 32

VICTORY!

At the top a hairy, bulky shape stands. As we watch, it laughs again. So hard that it doubles over. Hairy arms around its middle. Then with a defiant gesture, it stands to its full height. One of its arms rises to the sky amid the greens and reds of the Northern Lights. In its hand, a small reddish gold Feather flutters as if trying to take flight. The second Feather of the Phoenix!

Before our eyes, the hairy shape turns into a human. Behind him stands the Nylur. In one swift motion, he grabs the reins and jumps onto the back of the Nylur. With a final fist bump to the sky, he turns the Nylur around and is gone.

The Norse Star burns brighter and then fades to nothing. Overhead, a shadow passes.

It is as I feared. Evil has triumphed. These seekers have lost. The only good thing is that now the evil will leave my land. Now, my land must cleanse itself of the evil footprints.

CHAPTER 33

THE ᚲLEANᛋINᚲ

None of us move. Or speak. Our eyes locked on the top of Skogafoss. Tears run down my cheeks. I brush them away and more fall to take their place. Jerome's arm around my shoulders pulls me closer, trying to comfort me, but instead I find myself openly sobbing.

Jerome squeezes harder but says nothing. Looking at him, I see tears on his cheeks also.

"We've failed, Jerome. Failed the Atlantean Horse, Mneseus, and ... and Grandpa." I'm crying even harder.

"I know." His voice shakes so hard that he can't say any more.

"Do you think that because we don't want Grandpa to die, somehow we didn't search hard enough? That we somehow let the Horseman win?"

"No! No! We tried our best, Rosa. And in spite of the sorrow and pain that would come, we would never hurt Grandpa."

"There's something else, Jerome." I show him my hand. We watch as the burn mark continues to fade away, leaving only a minute scar.

"Did Mneseus bring us here? To Fail?"

I can't answer him.

Without warning, the ground above Skogafoss explodes into the sky. Water filled with rocks and ice bursts over the cliff top.

You must leave. Now! The island's spirits are sending the fire to try to burn out all traces of the evil.

"A volcano?"

Njal nods as the sky above us keeps filling with fire and rocks! From the top of the cliff, red fire races down. Red fire that boils the water it's using for a path. And ... red fire that is heading straight for us!

Njal turns and runs toward the ocean.

Grabbing Jerome's hand, we follow. Afraid to look back, we doggedly race as fast as possible, determined to beat the lava closing in on us. Heat and sulfur fill the air. If we don't find safety soon, we'll probably suffocate. If we don't burn first!

Abruptly, I stop. Jerome's arm around my chest holds me back as I struggle to break free.

"Rosa! Stop! Look!

CHAPTER 34

PAINFUL REMINDER

Two steps in front of me is nothing! I turn and push back against Jerome. OMG!

"What happened to the land? What about the volcano?" My eyes search around us. Nothing is the same except the waterfall. Its roaring presence the only reminder of where we were. The ground is littered with mossy rocks. Above the falls, the glacier fills the land behind.

"Where is Njal?"

Jerome starts to speak...

He is gone. Back to the past.

"How? Never mind..." Jerome says to the Atlantean behind us.

"Mneseus, we didn't get the Feather," I say.

I know. Now come. Take my hand. I will return you to your time.

"But what about Grandpa and the Horse?"

They know about your failure. There is no need to go there.

"But we want to explain. About the cat, the shapeshifter..." I say.

"Forget it, Rosa. He doesn't care why we failed.

Maybe because part of that failure is because of him. He brought us to the wrong place," he points accusingly at Mneseus. "Your failure cost us time, precious time that we needed to get to the Feather before the Horseman."

Mneseus says nothing. He points to our hands.

Reluctantly, we take each other's hand, and I put my free hand in Mneseus'.

The world spins around us, but I'm sure in that final second, I see the Norse Star fade into the brilliant red color of the Auroras. A painful reminder of our defeat.

CHAPTER 35

HOME

We're in my backyard. A little green. A lot sad and very disappointed. Jerome puts his hand on my shoulder, either to comfort me or to keep from falling down. I'm not sure which. I pat his hand and then sit down on the grass.

It looks just like when we left. Not much activity in the neighborhood or from my house. "Jerome, are you okay?"

He sits beside me resting his arms on his knees. "As okay I—we—can be. It's really just the same time as we left. Never would have believed it.

"And we didn't die, so you'll be able to go to practice."

Jerome gives me a shoulder punch. "Thanks for that, Rosa."

"You bet." I grin at him.

"You know, we have to call Grandpa."

"I know. Probably sooner than later." I squeeze my eyes tight to keep the tears from falling. "I don't know what to tell him, though."

"The truth. Grandpa knows this isn't going to be easy. He'll understand, I hope."

I nod and get up. "I'll be right back." Quietly I open the back door and go in the kitchen. My phone is still sitting on the table. No reason to take it with us.

"Good morning, Rosa." My mother calls from the living room. "You and Jerome are up early."

"Yes, we wanted to get in a short run before it got too hot. We'll be in the backyard."

"Sounds good."

A bit shaky, I go back outside and sit next to Jerome. "My mom's up. Wanted to know what we were doing."

"What'd you tell her?"

"That we went for a run before if got too hot."

He nods and takes my phone. "I'll dial Grandpa. It's getting close to evening there."

"Rosa, is that you?"

"No, Grandpa, it's Jerome. Rosa's right here beside me."

Jerome puts it on speaker.

"I'm here, Grandpa."

"Thank goodness you are both safe."

"But, Grandpa, we didn't get the Feather. He got it," I say, choking.

"It's okay, Rosa. You too, Jerome."

"We didn't mean to fail, Grandpa," Jerome adds.

"I know that. Somehow we'll get that Feather back."

"But how?" I ask.

"We'll figure that out, I promise. I'm just so glad you two are back home safe."

No one says anything for a minute or two.

"Grandpa," I say, "we love you."

"Yes, Grandpa, we love you."

"I know. It'll be alright. Somehow there will be a way. Take care of yourselves. We'll talk again later. I love you both very much."

"Bye, Grandpa," we both say.

"Goodbye. Remember, I love you both. We'll figure this out."

Jerome hangs up and gives me back the phone. He squeezes my hand. "We'll come up with something next time, Rosa. Just like Grandpa said."

"I know. I think."

THE END

MORE ABOUT

ATLANTIS

The Legend of Atlantis goes back thousands of years, maybe even before recorded history. It has fascinated explorers, researchers, and readers across the ages. To this day, explorers still look for proof that Atlantis actually existed. As for me, I firmly believe that all legends and myths have their origin in truths no matter how obscure the references. I chose the Mediterranean Sea as the location of my Atlantis because of all the mentions of this mystical place in the ancient literature. Some of the old stories told of an ancient race of extraordinary talented people who so angered their god, Poseidon, that he destroyed them and their island home. And as every good storyteller does, I've added my own ideas on the reason for that total destruction. If you're already familiar with the Atlantis legend, maybe you have your own ideas of where it was located. If so, I'd love to hear your ideas!

Write to me at *ccarpinello@mac.com*

CATS

Cats are welcome in Iceland. They get a bit of a bad rap because of the Yule Cat. In Icelandic myth, Yule Cats were said to roam the snowy land at Christmas time looking for humans to devour! We saw many cats in Iceland, but only in certain parts of the country.

As for cats with two different colors of eyes, those do exist. It's a rare genetic trait and usually occurs in white cats. The blue eye can be paired with a yellow, green, or brown eye.

FOUR HORSEMEN
OF THE APOCALYPSE

The story of the Four Horsemen of the Apocalypse comes from the *Bible*, specifically from the *New Testament* in the *Book of Revelation*. In The Atlantean Horse, Grandpa Simon simplifies his explanation for Rosa and Jerome like this:

First Horse—White (Rev. 6:2): *Conquering*

Second Horse—Red (Rev. 6:4): *War and Bloodshed*

Third Horse—Black (Rev. 6:5-6): *Famine and Economic Disturbance*

Fourth Horse—Pale (Rev. 6:7-8): *Death*

GYRFALCON

The gyrfalcon, the largest of all falcons, is a powerful bird of prey native to the Arctic. With its striking plumage – ranging from pure white to mottled gray – and fierce hunting prowess, it was considered the most prized raptor in medieval falconry. In the Middle Ages, gyrfalcons were reserved for royalty – only the king was permitted to hunt with these majestic birds, underlining their rarity and prestige in the courts of Europe.

In the first photo, my friend Wendy Leighton-Porter holds the Gyrfalcon. The second photo shows the

Gyrfalcon in all its glory. Wendy sent these photos for me to use. She is the author of the award-winning MG series *Shadows of the Past*.

You can learn about her and Max the time-traveling cat at *https://www.wendy-leighton-porter.com/*

ICELAND

Why Iceland? This island captured my heart and imagination even before I set foot on its shore. But why? Waterfalls! Waterfalls too numerous to count. Volcanoes! Real volcanoes cover Iceland. You actually walk on moss-covered volcanic rocks. Icebergs! Huge blue-tinted ice chunks floating out to sea. Glaciers! Long fingers of land, covered in ice, creeping across vast stretches of land as far as you can see. Beauty! Nowhere else have I seen raw nature in all its glory. Folklore! Many Icelanders believe in elves, shapeshifters, trolls, and other magical beings. I've been back three times and can't wait to go again.

PHOENIX BIRD

The Phoenix is one of my favorite animals right up there with the Unicorn. The idea that a creature must be consumed by fire to be reborn is mind-boggling and fascinating! Mentions of the Phoenix go back to ancient Egypt and possibly even beyond!

NORSE ALPHABET

ABOUT THE AUTHOR

Cheryl Carpinello started writing after she retired from teaching high school English. "There wasn't any spare time to write while teaching." In working with hundreds of students (ages 14-18) over 20+ years, she encountered many who didn't like to read.

After discovering the appeal that Arthurian Legend had for those students, she decided to write her own Arthurian stories for younger readers (ages 7-14) in the hope of stimulating their interest in reading. The tales from the ancient world also fascinated her high school students. Taking the myths and stories from those, she writes Tales from the Ancient World for PreTeen/YA. For those beginning readers, she writes the *Grandma/ Grandpa's Tales* series.

Cheryl's books have won numerous awards including the 2020 Moonbeam Book Bronze Award-Best Book Series Chapter Book for her *Guinevere Trilogy*. The *Guinevere Trilogy* also received the Mom's Choice Award in 2022. *The Atlantean Horse*, book 1 of *Feathers of the Phoenix*, was a 2023 Gold EVVY winner and a Readers' Favorite Honorable Mention.

FROM THE AUTHOR

I love doing classroom workshops for students, homeschooling co-ops, and kids' organizations like GSA, BSA, YMCA. We do Medieval Illuminated Poetry using the kids' original poems. Even the boys enjoy the poetry!

Contact me direct if interested at

ccarpinello@mac.com

www.ingramcontent.com/pod-product-compliance
Lightning Source LLC
Chambersburg PA
CBHW071358170626
46811CB00003B/1167